W9-BZJ-305

"I don't date, Sheriff Harrison."

"Look, about the kiss—I didn't plan that. That's not why I was waiting in the garage for you. I mean, you do eat, don't you?"

"Of course, I do. But you don't owe me anything. I was just doing my job today. I don't need any thanks from you. And I certainly don't want to be any more trouble to you. So, good night."

Mules weren't the only stubborn thing his folks had raised on their ranch. Boone pulled back the front of his jacket and splayed his hands at his hips. He didn't get why he was so attracted to this prickly city woman who had to be as wrong for him as his ex-wife had been. But he clearly understood his duty as an officer of the law, and as a man.

"You may not need any thanks, but I don't leave a lady in trouble...."

SADDLE UP AND READ 'EM!

Look for this Stetson flash on all Western books this summer!

Pick up a cowboy book
by some of your favorite authors:

Vicki Lewis Thompson
B.J. Daniels
Patricia Thayer
Cathy McDavid
And many more…

Available wherever books are sold.

www.Harlequin.com/Western

ACFEM0612R

⟨H⟩ HARLEQUIN®

INTRIGUE®

DELORES FOSSEN

BRINGS YOU ANOTHER DRAMATIC INSTALLMENT OF

When Deputy Mason Ryland rescues his new horse trainer, Abbie Baker, from an arsonist, he learns she's not only in Witness Protection and hiding from a killer but she's also been raised by Mason's father, who disappeared years ago. With danger drawing near, Mason and Abbie must solve an old murder and come to terms with a shocking family secret.

MASON

All secrets will be revealed this September 4!

Available wherever books are sold.

www.Harlequin.com

HI69638

JULIE MILLER

KANSAS CITY COWBOY

HARLEQUIN®
entertain, enrich, inspire™

If you purchased this book without a cover you should be aware that this book is stolen property. It was reported as "unsold and destroyed" to the publisher, and neither the author nor the publisher has received any payment for this "stripped book."

For Steve & Carolyn Spencer
Your dedication to the arts is such a blessing to our community.
You're smart, talented, generous people who've raised a
wonderful family and are fun to hang out with.
Carolyn, thanks for reading my books.
And Steve, we'll get you on a cover one day.

ISBN-13: 978-0-373-69634-5

KANSAS CITY COWBOY

Copyright © 2012 by Julie Miller

Recycling programs
for this product may
not exist in your area.

All rights reserved. Except for use in any review, the reproduction or utilization of this work in whole or in part in any form by any electronic, mechanical or other means, now known or hereafter invented, including xerography, photocopying and recording, or in any information storage or retrieval system, is forbidden without the written permission of the publisher, Harlequin Enterprises Limited, 225 Duncan Mill Road, Don Mills, Ontario M3B 3K9, Canada.

This is a work of fiction. Names, characters, places and incidents are either the product of the author's imagination or are used fictitiously, and any resemblance to actual persons, living or dead, business establishments, events or locales is entirely coincidental.

This edition published by arrangement with Harlequin Books S.A.

For questions and comments about the quality of this book please contact us at Customer_eCare@Harlequin.ca.

® and TM are trademarks of Harlequin Enterprises Limited or its corporate affiliates. Trademarks indicated with ® are registered in the United States Patent and Trademark Office, the Canadian Trade Marks Office and in other countries.

www.Harlequin.com

Printed in U.S.A.

ABOUT THE AUTHOR

Julie Miller attributes her passion for writing romance to all those fairy tales she read growing up, and to shyness. Encouragement from her family to write down all those feelings she couldn't express became a love for the written word. She gets continued support from her fellow members of the Prairieland Romance Writers, where she serves as the resident "grammar goddess." This award-winning author and teacher has published several paranormal romances. Inspired by the likes of Agatha Christie and Encyclopedia Brown, Ms. Miller believes the only thing better than a good mystery is a good romance.

Born and raised in Missouri, she now lives in Nebraska with her husband, son and smiling guard dog, Maxie. Write to Julie at P.O. Box 5162, Grand Island, NE 68802-5162.

Books by Julie Miller

HARLEQUIN INTRIGUE

*The Precinct
**The Precinct: Vice Squad
‡The Precinct: Brotherhood of the Badge
†The Precinct: SWAT
‡‡The Precinct: Task Force

CAST OF CHARACTERS

Dr. Kate Kilpatrick—Police psychologist and expert profiler. This cool, brainy beauty is patient, good with words and better with people. She's given the unenviable task of wrangling the visiting sheriff, whose private investigation is interfering with the task force's work. As the task force's press liaison, she's also the public face and spokesperson for the Rose Red Rapist investigation. But someone wants to silence her. Permanently.

Sheriff Boone Harrison—When his sister turns up as the Rose Red Rapist's latest victim, this small-town sheriff comes to the big city to get some justice. This rugged law-enforcement veteran is a man of action who can use a gun as well as he can ride a horse. He knows KCPD sicced pretty Dr. Kate on him to keep him in line and out of their way. But he doesn't mind the company.

Janie Harrison—The Rose Red Rapist's latest victim.

Flint Larson—Boone's deputy in Grangeport, Missouri.

Vanessa Owen—TV reporter covering the task force investigation. But is she after something more?

Robin Carter—Janie's boss.

Irene Mayne—Boone's ex-wife.

Dr. Fletcher Mayne—The new husband.

Officer Pete Estes—A young cop with KCPD.

Gabriel Knight—This reporter doesn't have nice things to say about the task force's investigation.

The Rose Red Rapist—His attacks have turned to murder.

Prologue

Boone Harrison never tired of standing atop the rugged Missouri River bluffs and watching the wide, slate-gray water thundering past. The dense carpet of orange, red and gold deciduous trees and evergreens lining every hill that hadn't been cleared for farming or cut out to put a road through blocked his view of the interstate and made him feel like he was the only soul around for miles.

Even though he was partial to the sheriff's badge he'd worn for almost fifteen years now, knew most of the folks in the tiny burg of Grangeport and on the farms and ranches in the surrounding county—and liked most of them—there was something peaceful, something that centered him, about getting away for a ride across his land on his buckskin quarter horse, Big Jim. Feeling Jim's warmth and strength beneath the saddle reminded Boone of where he came from. Smack-dab in the middle of the Missouri Ozarks, his family's home might not be used as a working cattle ranch anymore, but he rented out enough parcels of grazing land to a friend to keep it well maintained and looking like the thriving operation his father and grandfather before him had run.

Pulling his gaze from the early morning fog off the river some fifty yards below his feet, Boone nudged his heels into Jim's sides and cantered up over the rise toward the gravel road leading back to the house. A small herd of Herefords scattered as he approached the gate, and for a few mutinous seconds he considered chasing after them the way he had when his parents had been running the place. Give him fifteen minutes—twenty, tops—and he'd have them rounded up and on their way to the next pasture.

But they weren't his cattle. That wasn't his job. Boone was forty-five years old. His folks and his grandparents were gone now, and his brothers and sister had moved on. Buried in the county cemetery, married and raising kids in town, gone to the big city to make a career or simply thumbing their noses at ranch life. Boone might be the only one still living on the land where they'd all been raised, but he had other responsibilities now.

Leaving the cattle to settle back down to their sleepy breakfasts, he reined in Jim. "Ho, boy."

The big buckskin snorted clouds of steam in the chilly autumn air as Boone leaned over the saddle horn to unhook the gate. With the skilled precision of the ten years they'd been taking this morning ride together, Jim walked through the gate. Boone refastened it and, with nothing more than a touch on the reins, Jim trotted up to the road.

Boone had already noticed the tire tracks in the dusty gravel before he topped the next rise.

Company wasn't part of the morning routine.

Instantly on guard without making a fuss about it, Boone checked the gun on his belt, then pulled back the front of his jacket to reveal the badge on his tan uniform shirt. He adjusted his Stetson low over his forehead and rode the horse in to see who'd come out to the house so early in the day.

He recognized the green departmental SUV parked behind his black farm truck and knew the news wasn't good. Occasionally over the years, an inmate had escaped from the prison on the opposite side of the river, and his team had been put on alert. More often there was an accident on one of the highways that crisscrossed through town. Sometimes there was a drunk or a domestic disturbance, but his men could handle calls like that without his guidance.

This was something different. Flint Larson, the young man in the tan shirt and brown uniform slacks that matched Boone's own, stopped his pacing and came to face him at the edge of the porch.

Boone reined in Big Jim, and stayed in the saddle to look Flint in the eye. "What is it?" he asked, skipping any greeting.

They weren't so backward that cell phones and landlines didn't work out here. A visit to the house meant something personal. The pale cast beneath the deputy's tanned skin confirmed it.

"It's Janie." Boone's sister, the youngest of the Harrison clan. A failed engagement to the blond man standing on his porch, and the desire for something more than small-town living, had taken her two and a half hours away to Kansas City more than a year ago. "She's dead." Flint's voice broke with emotion before he steeled his jaw and continued. "The office just got the call from KCPD."

Boone crushed his fist around the saddle horn, feeling Flint's words like a kick in the gut. Janie? Hell. She wasn't even thirty years old yet. She was loud and funny. She had an artist's eye and the ability to put her four older brothers in their place. He needed to call those brothers. As the oldest, they'd expect him to take charge of making arrangements. Who were her friends in the city he'd need to contact? What the hell had happened to her, anyway? Driving too fast? An illness she hadn't shared?

He squeezed his eyes shut as the questions gave way to images of growing up in the house and town flashed through his mind. A lone daughter, spoiled by her parents and big brothers, overprotected, well loved. She could be just as rowdy as the rest of them, yet turn on the ladylike charm whenever...

The images froze and he snapped his eyes back open. Hold on. "The police?"

"Yes, sir." Flint shifted on his feet. He had to be feeling the shock and loss, too. "That's not the worst of it."

What could be worse than Janie's bright light being taken from the world?

"Tell me."

"She was raped and murdered."

Chapter One

Police psychologist Dr. Kate Kilpatrick shivered against the chill that lingered in the damp air and tightened the belt of her chocolate-brown trench coat as she hurried along the sidewalk to the crime scene. She hated being cold. And if this early October morning was any indication, then she was in for a long winter.

Impossibly long if she had to face any more visits to this revitalized area of Kansas City and deal with the job she'd been summoned to.

High heels, the KCPD auxiliary identification hanging around her neck, and the confident authority that she'd honed into a suit of armor over the years got the gathering crowd to part and let her pass with little more than a nod or a touch. She spotted the lanky, red-haired detective, Spencer Montgomery, who headed up the serial rapist task force she'd been assigned to, standing near the yellow crime scene tape that blocked the entrance to an alley between a local flower shop and a gutted warehouse building that was being remade into shops, offices and loft apartments. Summoning her courage on a deep breath, Kate turned off her emotions and braced herself for the death and violence reportedly on the other side of that yellow tape.

"Officer Taylor." She approached the tall, brawny K-9 officer who was guarding the scene with the proportionately big and muscular German shepherd panting beside him.

He touched the brim of his KCPD ball cap. "Ma'am."

She grinned up at him. The two had recently become acquainted with his assignment to the task force; as well. "I told you to call me Kate."

"If you call me Pike."

"Done." The nickname was unusual, but the charm was genuine.

The K-9 officer pointed to the trio of police officers conferring next to the wall at the edge of the alley. "They're over there...Kate."

"Thanks, Pike." She stepped around him and the dog to join the rest of the team. "Detective Montgomery."

"Doc." Spencer turned from the conversation he'd been having with his shorter, dark-haired partner and a copper-haired female officer she recognized as Nick Fensom and Maggie Wheeler, an investigator and a victim interview specialist also assigned to the KCPD task force. "The CSIs are nearly done processing the scene where the body was found, and we're conducting an initial canvas of the neighborhood." His report was as measured and concise as the tone of his voice. "Our Rose Red Rapist has stayed true to his pattern. The abduction occurred late at night after the victim closed up the shop for her boss—she was dead by two or three in the morning. This is the dump site, not where the assault occurred—and thus far we haven't turned up any witnesses." He handed over his notebook and let her study the observations he'd recorded. "You ready for this?"

"Not especially." She nodded a good morning to Nick and Maggie. She tipped her head toward the closed-off street behind her. "Is there any way we can thin this crowd out a little bit? And turn off the flashing lights? There's been enough speculation about the Rose Red Rapist escalating the violence of his attacks. All this commotion is only adding fuel to the fire of public panic."

"I'll take care of it," Maggie volunteered. She turned her mouth to the radio clipped to her jacket and started issuing orders.

"Thanks." Kate caught Maggie's hand and squeezed it before she could walk away, silently asking her former patient how she was handling the pressure of the unsolved investigation and the horrible memories the scene in the alleyway must have triggered.

"I'm good," Maggie reassured her, returning the squeeze with a real smile and reminding Kate of the engagement ring the uniformed officer now wore on her left hand. "It's the first time one of the assault victims has been found dead."

"Did you see the body?" Kate asked.

Maggie nodded, her smile fading. "That woman fought hard for her life. But I'm a fighter, too. Doing something to help put that bastard away helps me handle it all. So I'm good. We'll catch up later, okay?"

More friend than counselor now, Kate agreed. "I owe you a cup of tea. Give me a call."

"Will do."

Kate stuffed her hand back into the warmth of her coat pocket as the other woman walked away, and skimmed Detective Montgomery's notes before handing the book back to him. After discovering Maggie's affinity for understanding the victims of sexual assault, Kate's role on the commissioner's task force had shifted slightly. She wasn't a trained investigator, and she hadn't suffered a terrifying attack the way Maggie had, but she understood people. As a trained psychologist who counseled members of the police force and assisted with suspect interviews and criminal profiling, Kate knew how to read a face, a room, an entire crowd. She had a way with words—she knew when to talk, when to listen—and she knew what to say. In a city being terrorized by a serial rapist who'd reappeared in May after a ten-year hiatus, and had claimed his latest victim sometime last night, nerves were on edge.

It was her job to put those nerves to rest.

"I'm assuming you've moved the press to a neutral location?" She turned her attention to the two detectives.

Nick Fensom groused at the camera flash that went off on the other side of the street barricade. "Except for a couple of photographers trying to get a shot of the corpse—" he raised his voice to chide the photographer "—which we've already moved—"

"Nick," Spencer cautioned, quieting his partner.

The shorter man held his hands out in a begrudging apology. "The reporters are in front of the Robin's Nest Florist Shop, where the vic worked."

Just catty-corner across the street from where the previous victim had been abducted outside a local bridal shop. Kate nodded to the shop owner standing at the window of Fairy Tale Bridal, suspecting she and the other women who lived and worked in this neighborhood were beginning to rethink their choice of the trendy, upscale location. Two assaults in just six months—attacks that were brutal, traceless and now deadly—must be making every woman afraid of her own shadow, and every man look like a potential suspect.

Not to mention what news of another rape had to be doing for local business. With a determined intake of breath, Kate looked to her left, spotting the group of television cameras, broadcast vans, microphones and reporters waiting for her to make a statement on behalf of the task force. "I doubt the flower shop owner will be thrilled with this kind of publicity. I'll set up on the sidewalk facing north so the storefront won't be behind me in the picture."

"Good point." The detective reached out to stop a young officer who was assisting with crowd control. A sly glance at his navy blue uniform identified him. "Estes?"

"Yes, sir?"

"I need you to help Dr. Kilpatrick move this crowd of reporters down half a block or so."

"Right away, sir." The young man was barely in his twenties. He was new to the job and eager to please the senior officer. "Dr. Kilpatrick."

"Hi, Pete." She knew the rookie cop from a couple of counseling sessions on anger management issues he'd had that had carried over from his off-duty life into his work. "How are you doing today?"

"Haven't gotten myself into trouble yet."

"Good to hear." Kate summoned the necessary smile to send him on his way. She wore a more serious expression when she handed the notebook back to Detective Montgomery. "It's my understanding that the

Rose Red Rapist *hasn't* stayed true to his pattern. The woman he attacked is dead?"

Spencer nodded. "Blow to the head. M.E.'s office has her now. They'll have to tell us if it was intentional or the result of the struggle—maybe the vic saw his face or managed to get away, and he did it to stop her."

Two things that hadn't happened with any of the Rose Red Rapist's previous—surviving—victims. Changes in a perp's behavioral patterns could mean something as simple and tragic as silencing a witness to his crimes. But it could also indicate a psychotic break—a dangerous development that meant his attacks would become both more frequent and more violent.

Kate had counseled plenty of assault victims before, but she'd never been assigned to work on a case where the victim hadn't survived. "And we're sure it's our guy? And not a sick coincidence?"

The crime lab liaison assigned to the task force, Annie Hermann, approached the opposite side of the crime scene tape, holding up a bagged red rose in her gloved hand. "I don't know anyone else who leaves one of these with his victim. I'll run an analysis, but I'm betting it came from the flower shop where she worked."

"That's gutsy." Detective Fensom lifted the tape for the petite brunette in the navy blue CSI jacket to join them. "Buying a flower from the woman you plan to attack later? She probably looked him right in the face."

"Could be why he killed her," Annie theorized. After a moment's hesitation, she tucked her curly dark hair behind her ear and crossed beneath Detective Fensom's arm to join their circle. "Maybe he was a regular customer and she recognized him by the sound of his voice, even if he did wear a mask to hide his face the way his other victims describe. If she called him by name, that could have been her death sentence."

Kate offered another, more disturbing explanation. "Or maybe rape is no longer satisfying enough for our unsub to display his power over the women he attacks."

Spencer Montgomery tucked his notebook inside the front of his suit jacket. "Yeah, well, let's keep that tidbit of information to ourselves. The city's already on edge. If they believe it's a onetime thing, and not an escalation in the violence of his attacks, we might ease somebody's fears."

Kate nodded her agreement and inhaled another fortifying breath.

"Go work your magic, Kate," Spencer encouraged her. "You calm this chaos down and we'll finish up here."

"Right. We'll debrief later at the precinct?"

Detective Montgomery nodded. "This afternoon, if possible."

"Keep me posted."

As the detectives and CSI went back to work, Kate pulled up the sleeve of her coat to make sure her watch was visible. Short and sweet was the key to a successful press conference. She was already formulating a brief statement and would set a time limit for entertaining questions. When she was done, she'd send the press away to make their preliminary reports and tell the residents of Kansas City to remain cautious but not to panic—that KCPD was on the job. Then she could get back to her office at the Fourth Precinct to get some real work done on unmasking a serial rapist turned murderer and get him off the streets.

Kate raised her hands to silence the onslaught of

questions that greeted her and took her position on the sidewalk. She pushed aside a microphone that had gotten too close to her face and squinted as the bright lights of numerous cameras suddenly spotlighted her.

"Ladies and gentlemen, if I could have your attention, please." As her eyes adjusted to the unnatural brightness, some of the faces in the crowd began to take shape. She recognized Gabriel Knight, a reporter for the *Kansas City Journal* and one of KCPD's harshest critics. She knew Rebecca Cartwright, another reporter who happened to be the daughter-in-law of KCPD's commissioner, and who would no doubt put a more positive spin on things than Knight would.

She hesitated for one awkward, painful, debilitating moment when she spotted Vanessa Owen, a woman who reported local news for one of the city's television stations. Vanessa's caramel skin, dark brown hair and smoothly articulate voice had become a fixture on Kansas City televisions. She'd once been a fixture in Kate's life, as well. Vanessa had been a good friend, a sorority sister from college who continued to move in the same social circles as they established careers and marriages after graduation. The story between them that mattered the most had thankfully never been aired, though at times like this, the events that marked the end of their friendship still burned like a raw wound in Kate's chest.

But Kate was here to do her job, just as Vanessa was here to do hers. This wasn't personal. *Suck it up, counselor. You're in control here. KCPD made you spokesperson for the task force because they know you can handle it.* And with that mental pep talk sending her emotions back into the protective vault inside her, Kate blinked and moved on with the job at hand.

Beyond that first row of reporters, the lights and flashes and eager crowd made identifying others in the sea of faces nearly impossible. "I'm Dr. Kate Kilpatrick. I'm a police psychologist and public liaison officer with KCPD."

Gabriel Knight didn't wait for any further introduction. "Is it true that the Rose Red Rapist's latest assault victim is dead?"

Biting her tongue to maintain a patient facade, Kate looked straight into the reporter's probing blue eyes. "I will be making a brief statement on behalf of the department and the task force investigating the attack, and then I will have time for a handful of questions."

"Make your statement," Knight challenged.

Kate eased the tension she felt into a serene smile and included the entire gathering, including Vanessa Owen, in her speech. "A twenty-eight-year-old woman was sexually assaulted in this neighborhood last night, sometime between ten p.m. and three o'clock this morning. There was a rose left at the scene, indicating the attack was committed by the man—" she paused and held out her hands, placing the blame for their perp's notoriety squarely where it belonged "—*you* have dubbed as the Rose Red Rapist."

"Kate, is the woman dead?" Vanessa stole Gabriel Knight's question before he could ask it.

Although she bristled beneath her coat at the liberty her old friend had taken in addressing her by name, Kate merely nodded. "Yes. We are in the preliminary stages of a murder investigation—"

"Who was she?" Vanessa followed up.

"—and pending more exact information and notification of the family, I can't give more details at this time."

"Kate," Vanessa prodded. "You have to give us something."

She looked straight into the camera beside Vanessa. "This is what I can tell you. We *will* find this man. The task force members investigating these crimes are top-notch specialists—the best in KCPD. I guarantee that we will not rest until this attacker is caught and arrested."

A commotion at the rear of the crowd diverted Vanessa's and Gabriel Knight's attention for a moment, but the cameras were still rolling, so Kate continued with the briefing. "Rest assured that KCPD and the commissioner's task force are doing everything in our power to identify the attacker and ascertain whether or not this crime is related to the attack that occurred in May, or to others that have occurred in previous years."

The shuffling of movement and *Hey's* and *What the's?* in the crowd behind them finally garnered Gabriel's and Vanessa's attention, too.

The spotlight faded as cameras turned to see what the fuss was about. Normally, Kate was relieved when the cameras turned away to give her the privacy she preferred, but she had to say what she was required to say. "KCPD urges the women of Kansas City to practice common safety procedures. Don't walk alone after dark. Lock your cars and doors. Carry your keys or even pepper spray in your hand, and be sure to check under and around your vehicle before approaching it. Remember that KCPD is offering free self-protection workshops, or you can look into classes offered elsewhere. And finally we ask that everyone remain vigilant…."

Kate's voice tapered off as the lights followed the parting of the crowd, splitting like a crack in an icy lake, and heading straight toward her.

"Sir, you're gonna have to…" She thought she heard Pete Estes's voice, but it faded into the growing buzz of the crowd.

She spotted a cowboy hat and broad shoulders a moment before Gabriel Knight was pushed aside and a man dressed in a tan-and-brown uniform and insulated jacket stood before her. His eyes, dark like rich earth and shadowed by the brim of his hat, captured hers.

"Who are you?" Vanessa asked beside him. "Are you connected to this investigation? Has KCPD called in outside help?"

But the questions went unheeded as the dark focus of the man's eyes never left Kate.

"Are you in charge here?" His dark voice was just as coolly efficient, just as menacing, as the gun and badge next to the hand splayed at his hip.

Rarely at a loss for words, Kate cursed the splutter of hesitation she heard in her voice. But she shook off the foolish reaction and came up with a diplomatic answer. "I'm part of the task force that's in charge— Hey!"

Apparently, something she'd said was good enough for him. Immune to the flash of lights and uncaring of the public recording of the scene he was making, the cowboy closed his grip around Kate's arm and pulled her aside. If he hadn't been wearing a badge that identified him as law enforcement, Kate might have protested further.

"Lady, I've been driving ever since the report came over the wire early this morning."

"What report?"

With the interview effectively ended, she quickened her pace to keep up with his long strides. And though she tugged against his hand, his hold on her never wavered.

"What can you tell me about the woman you found in that alley?" he demanded.

"Excuse me, but we have rules about how a press conference is conducted here in Kansas City. We also have rules about interdepartmental investigations. If you need to speak to someone about a case, then you—"

"I'm only interested in this case." She nearly pitched off her pumps when he abruptly stopped to test the door on a nearby storefront. That same strong hand kept her upright and pulled her inside the boutique beside him, beyond the flashes of cameras and noise of the reporters and curious onlookers. Once he released her and shooed away the store clerk who offered to help them, Kate could face him. Only then did she see the jet-black hair with shots of silver at the temples. Only then did she clearly make out the chiseled jaw and six feet or so of height. Only then did she detect the scents of leather and man and some unnamed emotion that made her back up half a step.

"Who are you?" she asked.

This time, he answered. "I'm sheriff of Alton County."

Alton County? Central Missouri? "What are you doing here…?" Temper turned to confusion. She sputtered again while her brain shifted gears. "How do you know about the murder? We haven't even released her name to the public, pending notification of her family."

"You've notified them," Sheriff Cowboy stated. "My name's Boone Harrison. Jane Harrison is...was...my baby sister. I want to know who the hell killed her, and what you're doing to find him."

Chapter Two

Boone paused at the doors leading from the medical examiner's lab into the morgue and autopsy room. He pulled off his hat, working the brim between his fingers as he looked through the glass windows to the stainless steel tables inside.

He watched a dark-haired woman in blue scrubs and a white lab coat working beneath the bright lights at the middle table. She wore gloves and a surgical mask. And as she circled around the table, the front of her lab coat gaped open, revealing a baby bump on her belly.

But it wasn't the pregnant medical examiner who had his attention. He wasn't even shocked by the tray of wicked-looking tools or the cart filled with saws and hoses, glass containers and evidence bags.

Boone touched his fingers to the cool glass partition, wishing he could reach through the glass and erase the images before him. It wasn't his first dead body or even his first murder. But it was his first and only baby sister lying there—her life cut short, her beautiful laugh silenced forever.

His jaw ached with the tight clench of muscles holding back the tears and curses. And his gut was an open pit of anger, grief and failure, eating him up from the inside out.

"You don't have to do this, Sheriff Harrison." The firm, slightly husky tones of the blonde woman standing beside him filtered into his brain, tossing him a lifeline back to the reality at hand. Dr. Kate Kilpatrick stood shoulder to shoulder with him, viewing the same scene he was, maintaining a calm strength he couldn't seem to find within himself. "Certainly not right now. Give us some time to work first, and then I'll call you. I promise."

He flattened his palm against the glass and pushed the swinging door open. "I need to see her."

Startled, the medical examiner looked up from her work. She zeroed in on Boone and straightened to attention. "You shouldn't be in here. Hi, Kate."

"Sorry, Holly." Dr. Kate's hand on his arm slowed him a step, giving her the chance to reach the steel table before he could. "Dr. Holly Masterson-Kincaid, medical examiner. This is Sheriff Boone Harrison from Alton County." But she wasn't much of a wedge when it came to stopping him. Boone moved in beside her, looking down at the raven-haired woman on the table. "He believes the victim is his sister."

"Well, then, he really shouldn't be in here right now." The M.E. reached for the sheet draped at the foot of the table. "I'm just about to start… Hey!" She swatted Boone's hand from across the table. "Don't touch her. Please." She covered the body up to the shoulders as gently as if she was tucking a child into bed. "There may be evidence on her."

"I won't compromise anything."

"Sheriff?" He felt Kate's hand on his forearm again,

but there was more comfort than warning in this particular touch, and his gaze locked on to the elegant, pale, practically manicured fingers resting on his sleeve. "Perhaps we should wait outside and let the doctor work."

But he'd already seen the bruises on Janie's knuckles and the torn fingernails. He'd already noted the sticky-looking mat of hair beneath her head, indicating the blow that had ended her life. The worst of the bloody wound was hidden from view. There was nothing the M.E. or the police psychologist needed to hide from him. The loss had already imprinted itself in his brain, and deeper—in his heart. Boone's sister had been a firecracker in life. He couldn't remember ever seeing her this still, not even in sleep.

But the shell of the girl he'd grown up with was still there.

"It's her. It's Janie." He lifted his gaze to the moss-colored eyes looking up at him. But the emotion there quickly shuttered, neutralizing their color to a grayish-green before Dr. Kate pulled her hand away. With that unconscious bit of caring denied him, Boone cleared his throat and looked over at the dark-haired doctor. "Jane Beatrice Harrison. Named for both our grandmothers. She's twenty-eight. Born and raised on a ranch outside Grangeport, Missouri. Moved to K.C. about a year ago. She's single, but dating, I think. Worked at a florist's shop. Taught evening art classes at one of the community colleges here."

The M.E. picked up a computerized clipboard and started logging in some of the details he was sharing.

Boone's breath got stuck in his chest and he exhaled a big sigh before he could continue. "I talked to her on the phone just last week. But I haven't seen her since the Fourth of July. The family gets together for a big celebration—fireworks, food. One of my brothers has a cabin on the lake. She got a sunburn out tubing on the water with our nieces and nephew." Something numbing and merciless was eating its way through every nerve of his body, robbing him of rational thought. "Janie loved those kids."

"Is there anything else you can tell us about her life here in Kansas City?" Dr. Kilpatrick asked. "Any specifics about her daily routine?"

The answers drifted out of his brain. For a few moments, it seemed it was all he could do to stay on his feet and take in the world around him. Boone was aware of the two women processing everything he'd said. Holly Masterson-Kincaid was dark, dressed in white. Her hair was long and wavy and anchored in a ponytail at her nape. Kate Kilpatrick was fair, dressed in deep chocolate brown. Her hair was short and chic, with every strand falling into place. Both women were in their thirties, although he guessed the blonde to be slightly older than the brunette. Both women had their eyes on him, watching him with a mix of trepidation and concern. *Get it together, Harrison.*

Man, that Dr. Kate was a cool customer. He'd practically abducted her to get the answers he needed. He'd been bossy and on edge, yet she'd stayed calm and composed when she'd had every right to slap his face or call for backup to haul him away. She could have blown him off as the crazy out-of-towner stomping into their official territory, yet she'd answered every question with clear, if guarded, precision, and offered to bring him to the morgue herself.

Some part of his foggy brain knew she was probably running interference, keeping him away from the CSIs and detectives investigating the crime scene and talking to potential witnesses. But she could have called a uniform to drive him through town. She could have arranged for a receptionist to guide him down to the building's basement morgue. Instead, she'd volunteered to handle the ol' bull-in-the-big-city country boy herself. That took a lot of compassion, and probably more guts than the woman realized.

If Kate Kilpatrick could keep it together on a morning like this, then maybe he'd better do the same. With a nod that was directed to the highly trained law enforcement professional pushing its way through the emotions inside him, Boone summoned the detachment that had gotten him through a lot of disturbing crime scenes and graphic traffic accidents. "Has the body been cleaned up yet?" he asked.

The M.E.'s lips parted, in surprise, he supposed. But she set aside the computer pad and answered in a tone much less clinical than the one he'd used. "I was in the middle of processing when you showed up. If you'd given me some advance notice—"

"There was some jewelry she always wore." Boone brushed his fingertips against the collar of his shirt. "A necklace of my mother's. Three or four silver and turquoise rings she'd made. Janie was an arts-and-craftsy kind of gal. She took a jewelry-making class once."

The M.E. pointed to the paper envelopes and plastic sheaves on the table behind her. "The rings are in evidence bags, waiting to go to the lab upstairs. I didn't see a necklace. But there are clear signs of a struggle."

She looked back across the table to Kate, with a look

that could only be described as a plea for help. When Boone refused to budge, Dr. Kilpatrick nodded, giving her some sort of permission to continue sharing information with him. He needed to know everything—no matter how gruesome, no matter how tragic. His only solace right now was information—and the justice it would lead him to.

Resuming a mantle of detached practicality, Dr. Masterson-Kincaid pointed one of her gloved fingers at the thin, purplish-gray bruise bisecting Janie's delicate collar bone. "That would explain this mark. Looks like a chain around her neck was ripped off. Perimortem, judging by the bruising."

Another treasure stolen from his family. "Did the bastard take it as a souvenir?"

The blonde beside him shook her head. "That doesn't fit the profile. The Rose Red Rapist hasn't collected tokens in the past, but it is important to note. Maybe he overlooked it when he was cleaning up the scene."

"Back in that alley?" Boone would make time for a detour to search the place himself.

Kate shook her head and stepped aside to pull her cell phone from her pocket. "The body was found at a secondary location, like the others. But if we can locate the necklace, we might just find our primary crime scene." Her gaze slipped up to Boone, no doubt assessing how much information from their interchange he was taking in, as well as what he intended to do with that information. "Can you give me a description of the necklace?"

"A sterling silver locket. Heart-shaped, with a picture of our folks inside."

"I found a trace of some sort of metallic substance

in her hair—could be a piece of a broken necklace. I'll call Annie and Detective Montgomery to alert them to keep an eye out for it."

Dr. Masterson-Kincaid circled around the table, urging both her guests to clear the space around the examination table. "I'll give you some privacy while you're making your call. I need to take a break and phone my husband, anyway." She rested her hand on her belly and crossed to the double swinging doors. "Ever since we got the news about the baby, he's become a little more overprotective. If that's possible. Um." Boone glanced over his shoulder as she waited at the door to get his attention. "Take a few moments to grieve with your sister, Sheriff Harrison. But when I get back, I *do* need to get work. Alone."

"Thank you, ma'am."

"And remember, don't touch anything."

Boone nodded.

After the dark-haired woman left, Kate apparently decided to give him some space, too. "I'll go out there to make my calls, allow you some quiet time—"

"Don't." Not understanding the impulse, but not questioning it, either, he reached out and grabbed Kate's arm. He tugged her back to his side and turned, ignoring her startled gasp as he pulled her into his chest and hugged his arms around her. "Not yet."

"Sheriff, I…"

For a few moments, she stood there, rigid as a barn board, her arms down at her sides, her nose pressed into his chest. He knew he'd surprised her, knew he was taking liberties with a woman he barely knew. But he needed human contact right now. He needed the reassurance of a beating heart. He needed something strong to hold on to, something soft to absorb the pain and the rage and the grief roiling inside him that threatened to drag him down to his knees and bring him to tears.

As unexpected as the contact might be, there was a sensitive side to the police psychologist he must have tapped into. He felt her slender frame swell against him with a deep breath. And then she nudged her chin up onto his shoulder, wound her arms around his neck and stretched up on tiptoe to hug him back.

"Hush." She whispered soft words against his ear. Meaningless syllables that soothed him. "I'm so sorry, Boone. Shh."

Her body was flush against his, her arms around his neck and shoulders clinging almost as tightly as he held her. Boone buried his nose in the delicious scent of her honey-blond hair and let the grief overtake him in deep, stuttering breaths.

He held on as he purged the onslaught of emotion. Sensation by sensation, the blinding need eased and his body and spirit revived. Kate Kilpatrick was of average height, but the high heels she wore lengthened her legs and made her just the right size to fit against him like a hand to a glove. There was nothing remarkable about the shape of her body other than that the subtle curves were all there, in just the right places. She was a sophisticated blend of jasmine shampoo and woman and class.

She was businesslike yet compassionate, strong in body and resolve, yet she was the softest thing he'd held in his arms in a long time. At this moment, she was everything he needed.

But his timing couldn't be worse.

With something else waking inside him—something

that was more about family and the job, more about protecting one's own than it was about himself—his wants, his needs and the beautiful woman who'd assuaged them both for a few stolen moments—Boone pulled his hands up to Kate's shoulders and abruptly pushed her away.

He needed the chilly rush of air-conditioning filling the gap between them. He needed to see the self-conscious splotches of color on Kate Kilpatrick's cheeks. He needed to watch her straighten the front of her coat and tug the sleeves back into place.

He needed to see her fixing her personal armor around her so he could do the same himself.

"Sorry about that, ma'am," he apologized.

"Not a problem, Sheriff." She smoothed her short hair back behind her ears. "Sometimes grief can be too much to bear. And I was here."

"You've already done more for me than you should." And yet he had to ask her to do something else. As of this moment he knew Kate Kilpatrick better than anyone in Kansas City, now that Janie was gone. They were virtual strangers, yet she was the closest thing he had to a friend right now. She was also the best source of information he'd found thus far. Dr. Kate was a pipeline straight to the detectives who were working Janie's case. He glanced over to give his sister one last loving look, before facing the police psychologist's guarded expression. "I want to see the crime scene and any evidence your team has on Janie's murder and the previous rapes that bastard committed."

The green eyes blinked. Dr. Kate was shaking her head. "Sheriff Harrison…Boone…you need to take your sister home. You need to take care of your family right now."

He set his hat on his head, adjusting the crown to its familiar, comfortable fit. He closed his fingers around the crisp sleeve of Kate Kilpatrick's trench coat and the warmer, softer woman underneath, and walked her to the door with him.

Her psych degree and whatever heat was simmering beneath that cool exterior might have her programmed to be all touchy-feely with his emotions. But he didn't have the time to feel right now. "I need to work."

THE MAN PEELED OFF his shirt and tossed it into the hamper beside the socks and pants he'd worn last night.

His eyes were glued to the television across from his bed, and on the haughty blonde being interviewed on the morning news show. He paused, stripping down to his skivvies. The bitch was looking right at him, taunting him.

"We will *find this man. The task force members investigating these crimes are top-notch specialists—the best in KCPD. I guarantee that we will not rest until this attacker is caught and arrested."*

His gaze dropped to the bottom of the screen as the press conference was interrupted. He didn't really notice the cowboy or the commotion of wonky camera angles and muffled sounds as the reporters scrambled to pursue them. He was reading the words scrolling across the bottom of the screen—*Dr. Kate Kilpatrick, KCPD police psychologist and task force liaison officer.*

A shrink. He could just bet that woman wanted to get inside his head. Change him. Fix him.

A familiar resentment boiled inside him. *"We will*

find this man?" he mocked. "You wish. You've got nothing on me, woman." She thought she could threaten him, intimidate him into making a mistake. This one looked right at him and challenged him. Yet she looked all sympathetic, like she thought she could help him. Like he needed help. "I didn't do those things. There's nothing wrong with me."

Dr. Kate Kilpatrick was all blond hair and sharp tongue and classic beauty. She looked so much like *her.* She sounded like *her.* That entitled, smarter-than-him attitude was just like *her.*

Despite everything he'd done, despite the promises he'd made, *she'd* talked to him as though he wasn't good enough, as if he was some kind of broken thing that needed to be fixed.

The rage spilled over into his veins. She was trying to humiliate him. Publicly. Again.

A nagging voice of reason piped up in his head. *It isn't her. You know she's a different woman.*

No. Women like that were all the same.

He could feel the irritation crawling beneath his skin. They took. They demanded. They emasculated. If they ever deigned to notice him, that is. A woman like that—so confident, so beautiful—she'd look right through him. *You don't know that,* the voice argued. *Don't let her get to you. She'll make trouble for you if you let her get to you.*

"She won't get to me." He read the name scrolling across the bottom of the screen again. Kate Kilpatrick. She'd mocked him. Right there on television, for all the world to see.

He rolled his neck, scratching at the itch beneath his skin until he realized there was blood beneath his fingernails. Feeling the sticky stain on his fingertips more than the pain in his forearm, he dashed into the bathroom to check the mark in the mirror—to assure himself that *he* had put the mark there. There was no DNA that the brunette from the flower shop had taken from him.

He'd never make a mistake like that.

Breathing away the momentary panic, assuring himself that no woman had dared to get the better of him, he turned on the water in the sink and let it run hot before he picked up the soap and plunged his hands beneath the spray. After he'd washed his hands, using a brush to get rid of any trace of blood or skin beneath his nails, he opened the medicine cabinet. He pulled out rubbing alcohol, medicated ointment and plastic bandages to doctor the scratch he'd made, reveling in the sharp bite of pain that cleared his thoughts.

You were too smart. Too careful. The voice praised him, stroking his ego and fueling his pride. *You didn't make any mistakes.*

"Damn right I didn't." His heart rate slowed and his breathing evened out as the utter self-assurance of his actions returned.

Once he had finished doctoring his wound, he returned to the bedroom to remove the last of his clothes. Using his undershirt as a barrier to keep from touching any buttons, he picked up the remote and turned off the blonde liar and the morning news.

Then he stepped into the shower to clean up and get dressed for work.

Chapter Three

"You let Janie close up the store all by herself that late at night?" Boone braced one hand on the cash register and leaned over the counter at the Robin's Nest Florist Shop.

"I trust her with my keys. She's my assistant manager... Trusted. She *was* my—"

"After eleven o'clock? In the dark? Knowing that bastard was running around out there?"

"We close at nine p.m. Why was she here that late?"

"You tell me."

Boone couldn't keep the raw tinge of frustration out of his voice, and knew that the clipped tone and deep pitch and bulk of his shoulders were probably more intimidation than the brown-haired woman hugging the design book to her chest could handle. But damn it all, that redheaded detective in the suit had run him out of the alley where Janie had been found, and then set up a brick wall of a K-9 cop and his German shepherd sidekick to keep him away from the crime scene.

Normally, he was a patient man, a methodical investigator. But this crime burned far too close to the heart. His family was his responsibility, and he'd already failed if his sister had suffered so and ended up dead. He needed answers to why this unthinkable act of violence had happened—and he needed them sooner rather than later if he was going to have any chance of assuaging the guilt and rage and grief thundering along with every blood cell in his veins. If KCPD wouldn't let him comb through the crime scene with fresh eyes, then his next best avenue was to retrace Janie's steps yesterday and start talking to the people she'd had contact with.

The jingle of a bell over the shop's front door should have served as a warning to rethink this interview.

"We're closed today." The woman glanced at the intruder, maybe hoping for a polite escape, but the approaching customer only made him lower his voice and lean in closer.

"How long had Janie been working for you?"

The shopkeeper's blue eyes darted back to his. "Almost a year."

"And those were her regular hours? Did she close every night?"

"We traded off." She tried to look away again.

"Was it a regular routine? The same nights each week? Something that anyone watching this place for any length of time could pick up on?"

The blue eyes widened in shock and focused on him again. "I didn't realize I was putting her in danger like that. Yes, I suppose she'd had the same schedule for a couple of months—"

"Are you Robin?" Boone sniffed jasmine in the air a split-second before the softly articulate voice beside him spoke. The blonde in the brown trench coat rested a warning hand on his forearm, and the skin beneath his jacket danced at the unexpected touch.

Suspicion colored the shopkeeper's voice. "Yes?"

The lady cop psychologist who smelled better than any fragrance in the floral shop extended her hand. "I'm Dr. Kate Kilpatrick, KCPD. I'm a psychologist with the department and a public liaison officer."

The other woman set her design book on the counter and reached over to shake Kate's hand. "I'm Robin Carter. I own this shop."

Dr. Kate's steady voice and calm presence were quickly defusing both the florist's fears and Boone's own unthinking rudeness. "My colleague, Sheriff Harrison, here brings up a good point. For women, especially, it's smart to vary your schedule from time to time when it comes to personal safety. I know it can be hard to close the shop at different times, but don't work late every night, park in different locations, have someone meet you here from time to time, and so on." Perhaps sensing that he had a dubious control over his emotions again, she pulled her hand away and tucked it into the pocket of her coat. "People with predictable routines make themselves easier targets for a mugger or rapist to ambush."

The shopkeeper's skin paled beneath the blush on her cheeks. "I never thought of that. I'll make sure my entire staff knows. Thank you."

Boone's emotions might be in check, but that didn't mean he was finished here. "Ms. Carter and I were just having a little chat."

"Say, do you mind if I ask you a few questions?" Did Kate Kilpatrick just nudge her shoulder between him and the counter? Pushing him out of this conversation? Her move was subtle, putting a few more inches of protective distance between him and the woman he wanted to talk to. "Where were you last night? When was the last time you actually saw or talked to Miss Harrison? And was she alone?"

Fine. Questions he would have asked. As long as they got answered, he wouldn't nudge back.

"I had to leave early in the afternoon for a doctor's appointment." Kate waited expectantly—a patient ploy that often made a witness nervous enough to keep on sharing information to fill the silence. The woman had interrogation skills, for sure. Robin Carter tucked a lock of coffee-colored hair behind her ear and continued. "I was at the Lyddon-Wells Clinic. I've been going through in vitro procedures, trying to get pregnant via a sperm donor. You know, single career woman—biological clock ticking and all that. Yesterday the doctor called me in for a pregnancy report. Janie knew it was important to me, so she volunteered to switch nights with me. I left at three-thirty, and except for any customers she might have had, she was alone."

"Did you get the results you wanted?"

Robin hugged her arms in front of her and shook her head. "It didn't take this time, either. He suggested I look at adopting."

Boone didn't pretend to know about how a woman might feel if her hopes for a pregnancy fell through. His ex had put off starting a family year after year until he finally realized that she'd put their marriage on hold, too.

But apparently, Kate understood. "I'm sorry about the baby. Do you know who Janie was seeing?"

Boone tipped his hat back on his head at the abrupt change of topic. Catching the witness off guard was another smart tactic. He'd learned all the same interrogation strategies, but Dr. Kate's skills put his to shame today.

"No," Robin answered. "But I think it was pretty serious."

That was the first Boone had heard of a new man in his sister's life. Screw keeping his distance. He leaned forward again, his chest butting into Kate's shoulder. "Janie was in a serious relationship?"

The shopkeeper's gaze shot back to his, and Boone let Dr. Kate shrug him into a less-threatening position again. "She stopped talking about her love life, er, who she was dating, these last few weeks. Wouldn't go out for a drink with me after work anymore. Now that I think about it, she was secretive a lot lately. I'd interrupt a personal call and she'd quickly hang up. I invited her to bring a date to a staff party and she came alone. Left early, too."

"You don't have a name for this mysterious boyfriend?" Boone asked.

"I don't remember her ever mentioning it. And if he came to the shop, I never knew about it. She didn't treat anyone more special than her usual friendly self." Robin pulled a tissue from the apron she wore and dabbed at the sheen of tears in her eyes. "I'm going to miss that smile. Sorry I can't be more help."

Kate reached across the counter to squeeze the other woman's hand. "You've been a big help already, Robin."

Kate might be signing off on this interview, but Boone needed more. "Do you have any idea where she would have met this guy?"

For the first time during the entire conversation, Kate tipped her face up to his and looked him straight in the eye. Reprimand noted. And ignored. He opened his mouth to follow up, but Kate beat him to the punch. "I understand what you mean about devoting all that time to your career." He'd bet there was a kinder, gentler expression on her face when she turned back to the shopkeeper. "Other things get...overlooked." And then she was stepping back, nodding toward the front door. "Shall we?"

Boone ignored the unspoken command to exit stage right and pulled out his wallet to hand Robin Carter a business card. "If you think of anything, don't hesitate to call me...or KCPD," he added before Kate could correct him. He paused for a moment to tip the brim of his hat to Robin. "I'm sorry about earlier, ma'am. I'm a little upset today. But I appreciate your cooperation."

The woman sniffed back her tears and summoned a smile, appeased by the apology he'd owed her. "I can't imagine what you're going through, Sheriff. Janie was a sunny, vivacious spirit—and so talented. I'm sorry for your loss."

"You two were good friends?" Robin nodded. "Then I'm sorry for your loss, too. I'll send word about the arrangements for her services when I know them."

"I'd like that. Thank you."

Finally content to leave—for now—Boone turned to the door and gestured for Kate to precede him.

He'd barely closed the door behind them when Kate stopped in the middle of the sidewalk. She crossed her arms and tilted her face to challenge him. "You're going to scare away all our potential witnesses if you dive down their throats like that."

"I'm sorry if I scared the lady, but she had answers we needed."

"No, she had answers *I* needed. That the *task force* needed."

The lady's dander was up, all the way from the top of that honey-gold hair down to the soles of those ridiculously high, undeniably sexy heels. "Did Montgomery send you after me? I don't think your lead detective likes me," he asked.

Those mossy-green eyes held his for a moment before she turned and strolled up the street. "Where's your truck?"

Boone grinned behind her. Nice dodge. He'd take that as a yes, that Spencer Montgomery had called in cool, calm and eye-catching Dr. Kate here to corral him away from the investigation. He moved into step beside her. "How do you know I drive a truck?"

"You're a cowboy, aren't you?"

The muscles around his mouth relaxed with an actual laugh after too many hours of being clenched tight to stop up the emotions roiling inside him. He pointed a few parking spaces farther ahead to the black, diesel-powered Ford he'd driven in from Grangeport. "Yes, ma'am."

"I could tell that those boots weren't just for show."

Boone glanced down at the brown leather that was scuffed and broken in, and, okay, maybe tinged with a bit of the aroma that had driven his ex-wife off the ranch and out of his life. Although Boone hated to think of anyone as a stereotype, he supposed the Stetson and boots and badge stated exactly who he was, inside and out.

He wondered if the sophisticated facade and cool-as-a-cucumber demeanor said who Kate Kilpatrick was on the inside, as well.

Any curiosity about the pretty blonde vanished at her next comment. "The M.E. said she'll release your sister's body early tomorrow morning. Maybe you should be making those arrangements you mentioned instead of scaring away my witnesses."

He stopped beside the truck, his shoulders lifting with a weary sigh. "I can help. I've been at this job a long time and I know Janie better than any of you."

"I'm no rookie, either, Sheriff. I know Kansas City. And I know the Rose Red Rapist and how he works." She pulled a hand from her pocket and turned to face him once more. What was it about this woman's gentle touch on his arm that made each skin cell wake and warm beneath her fingers? "I'm also a psychologist. I've worked with several officers who've had to deal with the loss of a partner or a loved one, or even the death of a suspect. You need time. You need to grieve. You need to help the others in your family who are dealing with this loss, too." The warmth and subtle connection between them left when she pulled her hand back into the pocket of her coat. "Let us do this difficult work."

"Dr. Kate…." That's how he'd heard her introduce herself more than once, and that's the name that landed on his tongue. "I'm the oldest brother in my family, and our parents are gone. Janie was my responsibility. Finding who did this feels like my responsibility, too."

She nodded, perhaps understanding his guilt, or perhaps just eager to move him along out of the police department's way. "Please. Go find a hotel for the night. Did you come here by yourself? Is there someone you should call?"

Dr. Kate could maneuver a conversation six ways to Sunday, and a man had to stay on his toes to keep up—

or probe beneath that chilly control she maintained over her thoughts and feelings. He was interested in taking on the challenge, but right now he was too tuckered out emotionally to be a worthy adversary. So he relented and let her chase him off KCPD territory. For now.

"I'm a big boy, ma'am. Been taking care of myself a long time now." Boone circled around the hood of the truck and opened the door, but paused before climbing inside. "I'm glad Montgomery sent you to handle me. I'd have punched him by now."

Her chin tipped up as though his bluntness had taken her aback. And then her pink lips curved into a soft smile. "You're quite the charmer, aren't you, Sheriff?"

That glimpse of warmth through a chink in her armor made Boone feel like smiling, too. Yep, there was at least one thing he liked about Kansas City. He climbed in behind the wheel and started the engine. Then he pulled a contact card from his wallet and rolled down the passenger-side window to share one last word with Dr. Kate Kilpatrick of KCPD before driving away. "You need me for anything—you find out anything about this murder—I expect a call."

She stepped forward to take his card and it disappeared into the pocket of her trench coat along with her hand. "I will."

"See you later, Doc."

"Just one quote, Kate." Vanessa Owen had shown up at the precinct offices late in the afternoon, thankfully without her cameraman, and ambushed Kate the moment she stepped off the elevator onto the third floor. "I know we have history—and I know a lot of it was pretty bad—but this isn't personal."

"Nice speech." Kate took note of the visitor and press badges the dark-haired reporter wore around her neck, and quickly chucked the idea of having the doe-eyed beauty tossed out on her generous backside. Kate was in charge of public relations for the task force, after all. But that didn't mean she had to stand here and give Vanessa an exclusive interview when she'd already made a formal statement to the press earlier in the day. Skirting around the reporter, Kate headed for the temporary refuge of her private office. "If you'll excuse me, I have work to do."

When she turned the corner into the hallway leading to her office, a uniformed policeman with a buzz cut of brown hair jumped out of the chair where he'd been waiting and startled her. "Dr. Kilpatrick?"

"Pete." Kate pressed a hand over her racing heart and retreated half a step from the frantic young man who'd assisted her with controlling the crowd of reporters just that morning. "Do we have an appointment?"

"No. But my girlfriend called me at work and she said—"

"Pete." Kate stopped him before whatever the latest demand his girlfriend had requested of him turned into a full-blown rant. "I can't hold your hand through every crisis. Now we've talked about ways to improve your communication skills. Try one of those strategies to tell her what you're feeling. You have to practice them."

"But she said she'd leave me."

Vanessa invited herself into the conversation. "Officer, you interrupted us. I suggest you make that appointment."

"Vanessa."

"Five minutes of your time, Kate." Now Vanessa

was ignoring the young man altogether. "That's all I'm asking."

Keeping the irritation out of her tone, Kate patted the officer's shoulder, giving him a little encouragement. "Go on home, Pete. Talk to her the way we practiced. If it doesn't work out, I'll try to fit you into my schedule tomorrow."

"Thanks." He glanced up at Vanessa, then back to Kate. "Thank you, ma'am."

"You don't deserve five minutes." As soon as Officer Estes had disappeared around the corner, Kate resumed the walk to her office. "You can't talk to my clients that way."

"You were dismissing him already." Vanessa quickly caught up with her, refusing to be ignored. "Look, we are both professional women doing our jobs. Let me help you. Let me help the department's reputation—"

At that, Kate stopped and faced her. "There's nothing wrong with KCPD's reputation."

Vanessa arched a skeptical eyebrow. "You've been investigating the Rose Red Rapist for months—even longer, if the department's claim is true that he's the same man who committed a series of unsolved attacks and then disappeared for a few years." Vanessa pulled a phone from her purse and prepared to text whatever Kate might say. "Give me something to help calm the fears of the women in this city. I'm happy to give them your spiel about smarter ways to protect themselves. But my viewers want information about the crimes that have already happened, not just a public service announcement. They want to know KCPD is making progress. That there's hope the crimes will stop and that this deviant will be put away for the rest of his life."

"I hope you're not preaching gloom and doom to your viewers." Kate hiked her own purse straps higher onto her shoulder and unfastened the top button of her chocolate-brown coat, resigning herself to having this conversation. "Perhaps if you put a more positive spin on things, the department would be less cautious about sharing their information with you."

"I don't preach. I tell the facts. But I need some facts to talk about."

Kate glanced over at the late-afternoon bustle of activity in and around the detectives' cubicles. The door to the boardroom where the task force was gathering had already closed. There was no way she could indulge herself and pass off this inevitable chat with Vanessa Owen to someone else. She unfastened two more buttons on her trench coat, buying a few seconds to consider what she could say that wouldn't compromise the investigation, yet would get her onetime friend out of her hair. "You want facts? We're working on the serial rapist case, around the clock, utilizing experts from every department."

"Blah, blah, blah. That's rhetoric from the commissioner's office and Chief Taylor, and you know it. I want the scoop from the task force, from the detectives who are on the front line of this investigation."

Kate turned her head to the side and inhaled a deep breath to chill her temper. This woman had a lot of nerve. But she didn't get to ruffle Kate's composure. Not anymore. "Have you ever *not* gotten what you wanted, Vanessa?"

She could sense the let's-keep-our-personal-lives-out-of-it argument forming on the other woman's expression again. Kate didn't want to hear it.

"Fine. Just know that whatever I share with you I'll have to tell Gabriel Knight and the rest of the press following the investigation. The department can't show favoritism to one media outlet over another."

"Not a problem." Vanessa smiled and raised her phone again, apparently relishing the victory of besting a former sorority sister again. "I'm listening. I can still get my report on the late news. Knight will have to wait until morning for his paper to come out."

Funny how that competitive spirit had once challenged Kate to accomplish so much. And all the time she'd been busy accomplishing, Vanessa had been stealing behind Kate's back, having an affair with her husband, Brad.

Just give her a quote and get her out of here.

But while the embers of regret and resentment burned inside her, outwardly, Kate presented a few nuggets of information as succinctly as her position within the department demanded. "While we don't have a definitive suspect yet, we are developing a profile. He's someone local because he knows the city well enough to blend in or hide without drawing attention to himself. And he targets strong, professional women—whether they're up and coming or have already established successful careers."

Vanessa's thumbs hovered above her phone in mid-text. "So he's looking for women who are likely to fight back or who have the means to prosecute him should he ever be identified?" She resumed inputting Kate's comments into her phone. "This guy likes a challenge."

"Which is part of why he goes to such lengths to hide his identity and mask the site of the original attacks."

"Part of the reason?"

Kate checked her watch. Unless someone else was running late, Spencer Montgomery had already started the task force debriefing on the day's events. But leaving Vanessa with an unanswered question would only encourage the woman to come back.

She knew better than to publicize the unsub's penchant for sterilizing both the victims and the crime scene after the rape had occurred—that was a fact they were keeping to themselves to help eliminate bogus hotline tips and rule out evidence from assaults committed by someone else. But she'd probably already shared more of the profile than she should. She needed to be the stronger woman here and not let her emotions dictate her interactions with this particular member of the press.

"This is off the record because we don't have the proof yet…." She waited for Vanessa's nod of agreement before continuing. "But after careful study of the behaviors in each of the attacks, we believe our unsub has been hurt, humiliated, possibly even abused, by an important woman in his life. The assaults are a punishment, a means to…reclaim his power, to prove that he's stronger, smarter, than the woman who damaged him. Unfortunately, the attacks probably have nothing to do with the actual victims. In his mind, they all represent this one woman to him. He's proving to himself that she lacks the power to ever hurt him again."

At least Vanessa had the grace to look appalled and slightly terrified of Kate's description of the monster who was preying on the women of Kansas City. "And do you have a list of suspects who fit that description?"

But Kate had said enough. "I have a meeting to get to. If you'll excuse me."

With a noisy huff of exasperation, Vanessa fell into step beside her again. "That's it? Psychological mumbo-jumbo about a man you're no closer to identifying than you were five months ago?"

"We're making progress, Vanessa, but that's all I can share right now."

"Can I at least tell my viewers that professional women are more likely to be targeted than others? You're talking about assertive women—confident, successful women, right?"

Kate stopped and looked Vanessa straight in the eye. The implication was obvious. "Yes. Women like you and me."

After a momentary pause, Vanessa nodded. "Thank you for the insight, Kate. I'll share the warning, along with the safety tips you gave at the press conference this morning. I'm glad we can move past what happened between us and do what's right for the greater good of the city."

Well, at least one of them had evidently moved on from the tragic events that had ended Kate's marriage. Even though the humiliation and pain of just how she'd discovered Brad and Vanessa's affair had dulled over the past five years, a big scar remained on Kate's ability to trust in personal relationships. She certainly no longer believed in the friendship she and Vanessa had shared.

Without further comment, she turned her back on the reporter. Once Kate was alone in the empty hallway, her shoulders sagged with the need to catch a quiet moment to herself before she joined the task force meeting. She untied the belt of her coat and unhooked another button. The high heels would go next if she had another five minutes to decompress. But, "Oh, hell."

The door to her office was already open. Had she forgotten an appointment? She hurried the last few steps, then halted in the doorway.

"Oh, double…" She swallowed the rest of her unladylike curse as the sheriff with the coal-black hair unfolded himself from one of the visitor's chairs and stood.

"Dr. Kate." Holding his hat in his big hands, Boone Harrison nodded a greeting to her. With his insulated jacket draped over the back of the chair, she got a better idea of how broad shoulders and solid muscles filled out the dimensions of the tan-and-brown uniform he wore. The silver in his hair indicated he might be five to ten years older than she, but there was nothing over the hill about the fitness of his body, and he seemed as comfortable in his own skin, and as laid-back about the authority he exuded, as any man she'd met.

There was something basic and unpretentious about the masculinity imprinted in every rugged line, deep-pitched word and chivalrous gesture of Boone Harrison. And as much as his relentless and poorly timed refusal to leave her and KCPD alone to do their work annoyed her, she couldn't deny a rusty feminine awareness sparking to life inside her at every encounter with the man.

Taking a deep breath and forcing her weary muscles to smile, Kate unhooked the last button and shrugged out of her coat as she circled around her desk. She draped the coat over the back of her chair and smoothed the sleeves of her cashmere cardigan, diverting her focus to distract her traitorous hormones for a moment.

"Who's taking care of Alton County while you're here in Kansas City?"

"I've got deputies." A tall, broad shadow loomed over her as Boone approached the desk. "Since I'm staying the night to escort Janie home in the morning, I thought I'd check in to see if any progress has been made on your investigation."

She'd thought she'd gotten rid of him after their meeting at the florist's shop that morning. So much for a five-minute respite to recoup the emotional energy she'd expended throughout the day. After the long day she'd had—counseling a retired cop who was dealing with the recent death of his wife, as well as a young officer who'd been particularly surly about being assigned to temporary desk duty, observing witness interviews and trading carefully chosen words with reporters who were just as intent as Vanessa Owen to get the inside scoop on the Rose Red Rapist's latest attack—the last thing Kate needed was to deal with Sheriff Tall, Dark and Determined here.

Five minutes free from drama was apparently too much to ask for right now. Maybe if she quickly sent Boone Harrison on his way, though, she could at least close the door and enjoy two minutes of silence before joining the next meeting. "You've got a hotel room already? They fill up pretty fast this late in the day, especially south of town where the new crime lab and M.E.'s office are. Maybe you'd better—"

"I've got a room. But I'd sleep in my truck if I had to." A soft gray Stetson landed in the middle of her desk, followed by two broad hands braced on either side of it and the earthy, warm scent of the man leaning over them. Kate tilted her gaze up to a pair of whiskey-brown eyes that were entirely too close to hers. "Thought if I made an effort to be a little more civilized than I was this morning, you might be more inclined to share some information."

Didn't the man understand personal space? And had that breathy little catch of sound really come from her?

"You were understandably upset this morning. But that doesn't change the facts. You're out of your jurisdiction, you're too emotionally connected to the victim, and I don't have any details I can share with you right now." She slid a stack of files from beneath his hat and hugged them to her chest, straightening away from the desk and putting some distance between them. At least work was marginally less stressful than dealing with Marshall Hot-Shot here. She knew the expectations of her at KCPD. She knew what her clients needed from her. However, she wasn't as comfortable with persistent men and these flutterings of awareness. "I'm running late to a task force meeting right now."

"Perfect." He snatched up his hat. "I can sit in and listen."

"No." That had come out more aggravated than authoritative. She fixed a friendly smile on her face and tried again. "I've got your card. I'll call you when we're finished."

"Who was that woman pestering you out there?"

So was he truly observant? Or just plain nosy? Her arms tightened around the shield of papers she clutched to her chest. "A reporter."

"Did you tell her anything you haven't told me? I'm a cop and I'm family." Observant, she decided, reading the stern set of the lines beside his eyes. "I don't want to be surprised by anything I read in the papers or see on the evening news."

His reasoning made her stop and think. And relent. Her run-in with Vanessa had reminded her of just how frustrated and helpless not knowing the truth had made *her* feel five years ago. Boone Harrison wasn't leaving town until morning, anyway, so at least she could keep track of him and know he wasn't interfering with their investigation if he was in the room with them. That was how she'd present it to Spencer Montgomery, too.

"Fine. Detective Montgomery won't be happy about it, but I'll clear it so you can sit in and listen." Kate came around the desk, pointing a warning finger at Boone. "But not a word, remember? And anything you see or hear in that room has to remain confidential."

"I know how to keep my mouth shut."

Somehow she doubted that. But she only had so many fights in her on any given day, and this one was sorely testing her limits. "Let me go in and talk to Spencer first. This way."

"After you."

A half hour into the meeting and Kate wondered if she'd made the wrong decision. Although Spencer Montgomery wasn't pleased to have an unplanned visitor sitting in with the task force, he'd agreed that keeping the sheriff in sight was less worrisome than having him running through the city like a pinball let loose in a machine, conducting his own investigation into his sister's murder, impacting witnesses and giving off the impression that the task force couldn't get the job done on its own.

Still, it couldn't be easy, even for a veteran officer

of the law like Boone, to listen to the gruesome facts about his sister's rape and murder.

Spencer sat at the head of the boardroom table, his suit and tie looking remarkably fresh for this late in the day. He was speaking to his partner, Nick Fensom, a short, stocky, streetwise contrast to the buttoned-down task force leader. "Dr. Masterson-Kincaid says the traces of vinegar match what we found on his previous victim?"

"Yeah. The bastard cleaned her up after he raped her." Nick ran his fingers through his short, dark hair. "It doesn't make sense, though. If he took the time to get rid of any DNA after the sexual assault, then why leave the bloody mess we found when he dumped the body in the alley?"

Boone's hand fisted on his thigh in the chair beside Kate's.

"Nick," she warned, feeling the raging emotions coming off the sheriff in waves as he struggled to hold them in check.

"Sorry, man." Nick looked across the table and apologized. "I've got sisters, too. I get so angry when I see how he treats these women."

"You're an open book, Nick." Spencer chuffed his partner's shoulder in a masculine show of compassion. Then he steered the meeting back to the facts. "Anything else we can get from the M.E.'s report?"

Annie Hermann, the CSI attached to the task force, opened the folder in front of her and fanned out the papers and photos inside, digging through them until she pulled out a computerized sketch and set it on top of the scattered items. "I took pictures of the fatal head wound, and had Holly make a mold of the unusually deep wound track." Her dark eyes glanced up nervously, apologetically, perhaps, at the big man sitting between her and Kate. "Is it okay if I go into the details?"

The tension in Boone never eased, but he turned his head toward the petite woman beside him. "Do it."

After a murmured apology, Annie continued. "Holly says the blunt-force trauma was definitely the COD. But what he hit her with isn't immediately apparent. It's almost as if she was impaled by something. Nothing I found at the dump site seemed to fit. Of course, that's not the primary crime scene, either. I plan on going through our database and running simulations to figure out what kind of tool or instrument made that wound."

Spencer nodded. "Let us know as soon as you determine the weapon. If it's something unusual, maybe specific to a certain profession, that could help narrow our suspect and crime scene searches."

"Will do."

Boone's eyes remained transfixed on the drawing. Thankfully, it wasn't an actual picture of his murdered sister. Kate was about to warn Annie to pick up her mess, or act on the impulse to give Boone's fist a supportive, sympathetic squeeze beneath the table herself, when he reached for something else from the stack in front of Annie.

He picked up an 8 x 10 photograph and studied the jewelry displayed beside the cataloging number in the picture. Kate leaned forward, watching his eyes narrow in concentration. She quickly sat back when he turned his focus past her to where Spencer Montgomery sat at the head of the table. "May I comment, Detective?" he asked.

"If you can tell us something new." Spencer seemed

wary of inviting Boone into the discussion. But he was too smart a cop to overlook a possible lead, even if it did come from someone outside the task force. "We've all got a description of the necklace you said was missing."

"It's not that. All this other jewelry, this handmade silver and turquoise stuff—I've seen Janie wear it." He pointed to the smallest round object in the photo. "But this ring is something new."

Kate pulled the photo in front of her to study the jewelry in question. "A ruby and diamonds set in white gold? A lot of diamonds. That's expensive."

When Maggie Wheeler, the red-haired police officer sitting opposite her, asked to see it, Kate slid the photo across the table. "It looks like an engagement ring." She twirled her left hand in the air to show off the simple solitaire set in gold that she wore. "I saw designs like that when John and I were shopping."

"Was your sister engaged?" Spencer asked, studying the photo himself as it made its way around the table.

"No."

"In a relationship?"

Boone shook his head. "Nothing serious enough to warrant a gift like that. At least not that I knew of."

Feeling the subtle shift from helpless anger to focused purpose from the man beside her, Kate voiced the information Boone was probably already sorting through inside his head. "Robin Carter, the victim's boss, at her shop this morning said she thought Janie had been unusually secretive lately. And that she'd stopped dating."

Spencer's sharp gray eyes challenged Boone. "Could she have been involved with someone she didn't tell you about, Sheriff?"

Annie tucked a curly dark lock behind her ear. "Not every woman confides in her family when she's in a relationship."

Nick Fensom scoffed at the notion of a woman keeping her mouth shut. "My sisters do. Sometimes, I can't shut 'em up about the latest stud or hottie or whatever name they're calling them."

"Really?" Annie bristled at the amusement in Nick's tone. "Women with good sense confide in you?"

"My family's close, Hermann. We talk." He shrugged off her sarcasm and leaned back in his chair. "Unless the guy's trouble. And then they keep it a secret because they know I'll check him out—and run him off if he's no good."

Unless the guy's trouble. Even Nick went silent at the implication of what he'd just said. The words hung in the air around the table, and a group decision was silently made.

Nick groaned. "She would not have been dating our unsub, would she?"

"You said this guy was faceless in the city," Boone reminded him, "that he blends in so well that no one suspects him of being *no good.*"

"Thank you for the heads-up, Sheriff." Spencer closed the folder in front of him and stood, dismissing them all to do their work. "Let's find out who Jane Harrison was seeing."

Chapter Four

"Dr. Kate—do you have a minute?"

"Sorry, no."

"Coward." Even now, Kate could recall the expectation she'd read in Boone Harrison's warm brown eyes before she'd turned her back on him and scurried down the hallway to her office where she'd closed the door... and locked it. "No," she insisted to herself, not bothering to stifle the yawn that stretched nearly every muscle in her face. "You're a survivor, Kate. You did what was necessary to get through this day."

After saving the notes she'd been typing up on her laptop, Kate slipped off her pumps and curled her cramped toes into the carpet beneath her desk. She'd stayed at the office far longer than she'd intended. But once the duty shift had changed on the main floor and the buzz of voices diminished, she'd finally found the calming quiet and solitude she needed to recharge her batteries and prioritize the demands on her time and emotional energy once again.

As the task force meeting ended, she knew that Boone Harrison had wanted to say something more to her. Maybe he was even going to ask her to dinner so he could continue grilling her for answers to his sister's murder. Or maybe he simply wanted to pass the time with the most friendly face he'd found in Kansas City so that he wouldn't have to be alone with his thoughts and his grief the rest of the night.

But she'd reached the limits of patience and compassion for one day. The man had barged into her well-ordered life, bullied his way past her personal defenses, and tapped into a dangerously unreliable part of her psyche—her heart.

The counselor in her was inclined to listen to his helplessness and anger. The woman in her wanted to ease the guilt and grief that was almost too much for even a strong, mature man to bear. But she had to handle this investigation with her brain, not her heart. She had to manage her life with the same strict logic.

Caring led to vulnerability.

Vulnerability made her an easy mark for heartbreak and betrayal.

Forgetting either of those two truths would lead Kate down the same path that had nearly destroyed her five years earlier.

She'd known Boone Harrison for only a day—he didn't even qualify as a friend. She owed him nothing beyond the professional courtesy extended to him by the department. And as much as part of her wanted to help him get through not just this day but also the ongoing adjustments he'd face after losing someone he'd been so close to, Kate was too smart to let things with the sheriff get personal and make a mistake of the heart again.

So she'd left her coworkers behind. She'd sent Boone on his way with a smile and the very real excuse that she still had work she needed to complete before her day ended.

Now, with only the lamplight over her desk and the words on the laptop screen to keep her company, Kate wondered at the emptiness she'd chosen for herself in the name of emotional survival. She'd certainly never advise one of her clients to handle hurts and disappointments this way. But that was the point, wasn't it? She couldn't take on the issues of all her clients and visiting sheriffs, manage the image of the task force, reassure the frightened citizens of an entire city *and* deal with drama in her own life without losing her patience, draining her compassion, blowing out a few brain cells and winding up being no good to anybody. She had to protect herself like this, right?

Made sense.

Maybe she could dispel this unfortunate case of second-guessing her choices today by conducting a little exercise she sometimes used with clients who bottled up or misdirected their emotions.

Kate raised her arms over her head and extended her legs, stretching out the kinks in her body from head to toe before collapsing back into the chair with a weary sigh. She imagined how her impromptu interview with Vanessa Owen might have gone if she didn't exercise such self-control.

"Get out of my face, you witch. You've already taken enough from me. You won't get another damn thing out of me."

"I'm only doing my job, old friend. Please help."

"You already helped yourself to my husband. Your treachery killed him. You killed my marriage, my abil-

*ity to trust and did serious damage to my self-esteem.
You don't get to ask for favors from me."*

*"You were a fool not to know what was going on,
Kate."*

*"Maybe. But I learned to never be made a fool of
again."*

Feeling a bit of satisfaction, Kate nodded. That was
closer to what she'd really wanted to say to Vanessa
Owen.

And how could she have handled Boone Harrison
differently? Spared herself the full-body hug and dark
eyes that penetrated her emotional armor and awoke
something tingling and feminine and needy inside her?
How should she have reminded herself that it was duty,
not compassion, that had forced her to accept his company so many times today?

"Get your hands off me, you clod."

"But you like it when I put my hands on you."

Kate startled in her chair and sat up straight, glancing around her office as though the words had been real
and spoken out loud for the wrong person to hear. She
was supposed to be purging her resentment and frustration, reclaiming control of her emotions. This wasn't
the time to indulge a subconscious admission. She had
enough conflict battling it out in her head without inviting a latent sexual attraction into the mix.

"Try again," Kate advised herself. She inhaled a
cleansing breath and replayed this morning's press
conference in her mind, envisioning what she should
have said to the buttinsky sheriff who'd demanded answers from her.

*"Handle your own problem, cowboy. I have a job
to do."*

Better. Maybe she should have sicced Boone and Vanessa on each other, and then half the stresses of Kate's day would have become someone else's. After a brief introduction, Kate could have slipped away. Boone would have politely stood, and removed or tipped his hat when Vanessa entered the room. Vanessa would have been charmed by the old-school chivalry. And then she'd have tried to take advantage of it. She'd appreciate an interview with a family member of the rapist's latest victim. She could exploit Boone's unsanctioned investigation to attract viewers and ratings.

But Boone was more cop than country bumpkin. He'd be too smart to be taken in by Vanessa's charm. Vanessa would be intrigued by a challenge like that. Kate could visualize the sheriff and the reporter strolling off together, each primed for a battle of wits and will while Kate sat alone in her office, oblivious to the secret alliance, just as she'd been oblivious to Brad and Vanessa's affair until the police had called about the heart attack in his mistress's bed....

Kate swore at the unsettling turn of her thoughts. "End the damn exercise, already."

She rolled her chair back in front of her laptop, typing in a few more words before an unexpected revelation from the mental exercise gone wrong popped into her head. "They'd keep their relationship hidden from me," Kate murmured out loud.

She flashed back through her day—Robin Carter's speculation that Janie Harrison had been seeing someone, the picture of a very expensive ring, changes in behavior, unexplained gifts—secrets that neither family nor close friends knew.

In hindsight, Kate recognized the similarities from her own past.

"Jane Harrison was seeing a married man. Or possibly a student—someone she'd get in trouble over for having a relationship with." Although a student was less likely to have the money for that ruby and diamond ring—unless he'd come from a wealthy background or had stolen it. And a thief wouldn't take that necklace and leave all those rings behind. All were specific leads the team could look into.

Energized by the possibility of narrowing down their suspect pool, and welcoming the distraction to the wayward turn of her thoughts a moment earlier, Kate turned to her desk computer and typed her suspicions and reasoning into an email and sent it to the other task force members. Then she pulled out a phone book and put in a call to the community college where Jane Harrison had worked.

Although evening classes were in session, she discovered that the business offices had already closed for the day. Ignoring her frustration over the delay in getting some answers, she gathered her thoughts and left a succinct message on the line for the director of the Fine Arts department: "…that list should have class rosters, departmental colleagues—anyone she might have come into contact with on campus. You can reach me here at KCPD, or on my cell if I'm out of the office, to arrange a meeting to go over the information. Thank you."

Feeling reenergized by that bit of deductive reasoning and the small but potentially significant breakthrough she'd just made on the case, Kate decided it was time to call it a night. The clock on her wall and the rumbling in her stomach confirmed it. She slipped her swollen toes back into her high heels, packed her laptop into her shoulder bag, pulled on her trench coat and shut off the lights.

This day was done. Soup and salad, a steaming hot bath and one of the food shows she liked to watch on television were waiting for her at home.

After checking out with the overnight desk sergeant, Kate rode the elevator down to the first floor and stepped outside. The cool autumn air whipped her hair into her face. She paused on the entryway's top step to brush her bangs off her forehead and blink the grit carried by the wind from her eyes.

A glimpse of movement, of someone more shadow than substance, darted beyond the limestone railing and vanished out of sight. Kate's breath jolted through her chest. She captured her hair behind each ear and turned her face away from the swirling air currents that promised rain, peering into the night to double-check what she'd seen. It was probably someone taking a shortcut through the grass or hugging the building to avoid the battering wind blowing from the north.

But a closer look revealed no one, nothing, stirring besides the crispy, thinning leaves on the trees lining the sidewalk, and the swaying steel and flickering illumination of the street lights and traffic signals nearer to the street.

Irritated with how easily she'd been startled, Kate relaxed with a cautious sigh, and she cinched her coat more tightly around her waist. Fatigue had made her senses unreliable, she reasoned silently. She'd seen the shadow of a branch or a bobbing circle of light from the corner of her eye and mistaken it for something more sinister.

She'd been profiling too many suspects lately. With a shake of her head, she crossed down the wide stone steps to the sidewalk. She swept her gaze from side to side as she walked down to the street light at the corner, alert to any other signs of movement. But she doubted she'd see anything unless her imagination conjured it. There weren't many cars heading downtown past precinct headquarters, and even fewer pedestrians on the block.

If she'd left when the shift had changed three hours earlier, the sidewalks on either side of the street would be filled with coworkers heading for home or a night out on the town. With the threat of rain driving everyone indoors as quickly as possible, there were only a few other brave souls out and about, carrying briefcases and backpacks, hunched down against the wind as they hurried from the government buildings, courthouses and legal offices in the area to their cars or the nearest bus stop.

"Smooth move, Doctor," Kate chided herself. Her heels clicked against the concrete, echoing her increasing heart rate as she neared the crosswalk that would take her to the parking garage across the street. She deserved the little rush of nerves that quickened her pace. She hadn't even followed her own safety advice that she'd given to the women of Kansas City that morning. She was alone. After dark. Walking to her car in the same garage where she'd been parking for years. Not smart. With a serial rapist turned killer hiding on the streets, was it any wonder she'd been able to spook herself with nothing more than wind and shadows? "Real smooth."

But surely this wasn't a terrible risk. The parking garage was across from a police station. The street lamps might be undulating in the wind, but they were working. And even though she fit the profile of the women he attacked, this wasn't the neighborhood where the Rose Red Rapist had abducted his last two victims.

Still, she was more than uncomfortably aware of the man in dark brown coveralls approaching the same intersection from one of the side streets. He wasn't any taller than she, but from this angle, most of his face was obscured by the sweatshirt hoodie he wore beneath the insulated jumpsuit. Kate made a point of standing in the circle of lamplight as he joined her to wait for the traffic signal to change. For a split second, she considered crossing against the light, but, like Murphy's Law, the traffic that had seemed so sparse a few moments ago now showed up with three cars and a truck to keep her on the sidewalk.

She was vaguely aware of the man glancing in her direction, but studiously kept her eyes focused on the traffic in front of her. "Looks like a storm's coming," he said politely enough, his voice a gravelly whisper.

Kate nodded, sidled half a step closer to the streetlight, then stepped off the curb as soon as the vehicles had cleared the intersection. Either put off by her lack of a response, or waiting for the light to change, the man held back while she darted across the street. She'd already circled around the crossbar gate at the garage's entrance when she looked back to see the man step onto the sidewalk behind her and turn toward the open-air parking lot just south of the parking garage.

Expelling her paranoia on a relieved sigh, Kate hurried to the elevator and pushed the call button. She was grateful to see the doors open immediately and that the car inside was empty. She stepped inside and pushed the button for the sixth floor.

"Dr. Kilpatrick?"

Not Pete Estes again. Resentment fisted in her chest. The kid needed to grow up.

"Hey! Wait!"

Kate pushed the Door Close button. Not the most professional of responses, but she just couldn't deal with his issues and hold his hand right now. She'd already gotten her nerves worked up with the man at the corner. She wouldn't be a very patient listener right now, anyway.

"Dr. Kate!"

She might have heard someone calling her name again, might have imagined the muted crunch of quick footsteps over the concrete. But when a dark blur of shadow rushed toward the elevator, she gripped the side railing and punched the Door Close button over and over, speeding the process to be alone and safe inside the elevator.

She didn't imagine the deep-pitched curse before the doors squeezed shut.

"Pete," she sighed at the young man's desperation to save his relationship with the girl he'd gotten pregnant. Kate couldn't be sure if those footsteps had changed course to take the stairs, or if that was her own pulse hammering a warning signal in her ears. Either way, her brain had kicked into overdrive, driving out both pity and fatigue.

She was embarrassed to realize she hadn't given better thought to her own safety at this time of night. It worried her to think the man outside the elevator had truly meant her harm. Would Pete Estes really turn his temper on her? Or maybe it hadn't been her client at all.

Her name had been splashed all over the television and papers this morning. She was a fixture in the department. A lot of people knew her name.

Was it possible for the man in the coveralls to keep to the shadows and move quickly enough that he could have been the movement she'd spotted beside the precinct's front steps, the stranger at the street corner *and* the man rushing up inside the parking garage? Surely, he'd have to fly like the wind gusting outside in order to be in all three places. And maybe she was believing the worst of an innocent man—or two innocent men—or even three—when each encounter could be explained away by coincidence, regret at the chance she'd taken by walking out here alone and her overly analytical way of thinking.

Nonetheless, Kate had her keys out and her pepper spray in hand when the elevator reached the sixth level and the doors opened. She heard an engine gunning somewhere in the distance. But that wasn't the noise that alarmed her.

"Oh, no." Did she trust that coincidence could also explain away the footsteps she heard coming up the stairs behind her?

Chances were, someone whose legs were fueled by the aggravation of missing the elevator was climbing his way to one of the garage's upper levels. Or maybe a reporter had been lying in wait, ready to ambush her with questions the way Vanessa Owen had. If the man was half as determined as Vanessa, he wouldn't let six flights of stairs deter him from getting his story. Of course, there was Pete. And the man in the coveralls.

And the sound of an engine speeding up and circling through each level of the parking garage beneath her feet.

Maybe she'd been foolish to reason away those instincts that warned her to be wary of any man approaching her at this time of night.

Kate spotted her Lexus against the far wall and quickened her steps. Normally, she didn't park so far away, but the garage had been nearly full when she'd returned for the task force meeting that afternoon. Now, there were a handful of cars to the left and right, but hers sat at the end of the row, facing away from her. So very far away.

The timbre of each footfall changed as the man behind her left the steel grate stairs and followed her onto the solid concrete of the parking level.

Followed her?

Squeezing the pepper spray in her fist, Kate broke into a run.

She'd covered the length of the garage before she realized that the pattern of footsteps behind her hadn't changed. She was running, but the man behind her wasn't. Kate halted at the trunk of her car and whirled around.

Her words came out in breathless derision. "Stupid woman. You stupid…freaked-out…"

The man hadn't followed her at all. In fact, he was nowhere to be seen. He must have veered off into another parking lane and hadn't been after her at all. Danger wasn't closing in on her. She was just letting her emotions spin her imagination into overdrive.

Cursing the pinch of her shoes and her readiness to believe the worst of the men in the world around her tonight, Kate tapped the remote to unlock her car. She tugged the strap of her purse back over her shoulder, opened the car door and froze.

The man in the coveralls might not be chasing her. There might not be any client or reporter in hot pursuit. But someone definitely had her in his sights.

The squeal of tires over the pavement barely registered as she moved around the open door to read the message scrawled across her windshield in bright red.

Lies, Kate. Lies! was all it said.

And the wilted red rose tucked beneath a wiper blade left no doubt who the message was from.

"Please be paint." She reached out to touch one finger to the sticky exclamation point. Her stomach plummeted as she quickly pulled back, rubbing the vile evidence across her fingers in her efforts to get rid of it. There was no way to know if it was human or not, but she was 99 percent sure it was blood.

"I don't understand." Shock dampened her hearing to the noises around her. She tried to force logic into her brain, tried to make sense of a bloody threat that didn't fit the profile of the opportunistic rapist the task force was after. How had he found her? What connections did he have, how long had he watched, to know this car was hers? What did the message mean?

Why was she still standing here, contemplating this frightening mess?

Kate took a step back, then another.

A hand closed over her shoulder and she screamed.

"WHOA, WHOA, WHOA." Boone deflected the stinging attack of pepper spray as Kate spun around, twisting her wrist and knocking the vial to the concrete. "Kate." The canister rolled out of sight beneath her car and she came back swinging. He caught that hand, too, and pinned it against his chest, willing her to see through her panic and identify him. "Kate! It's me. Boone."

"Boone?" Her hands balled beneath his, curling into the front of his jacket.

"Yeah. Pain in the butt? Won't go away?" Now that the weapon was gone and the fists were accounted for, he eased his defensive hold on her. "Sorry I startled you, but you didn't hear me. I tried to catch you on your way into the garage, but your mind was someplace else."

Apparently it still was. That soft green gaze bounced from his chin to his chest and up to the brim of his hat before meeting his. "What are you doing here?"

Now, what would make a sensible woman take off running like that? What would put that dazed look in her eyes?

"I was parked outside on the street. I've been waiting for you to get off work." He dropped his voice to little more than a whisper, hushing her the way he'd croon soft words to a skittish colt. "I saw you were walking to your car by yourself and I tried to catch you, but you took off. I thought I'd better grab my truck and find out where you were parked before I missed...oh. Okay."

One second she was staring at him as if he was talking gibberish, the next she was walking into his chest, latching on with a death grip that pinched the skin beneath his uniform.

"You're shaking like a leaf." Boone had no problem wrapping his arms around her and resting his chin against the silky crown of her hair. He did have a problem with the clammy chill of skin he felt at her nape. He had a very big problem with the vandalism he spotted on her windshield when he sought out an explanation for Kate Kilpatrick's uncharacteristic display of confusion and vulnerability. "Come here."

That she willingly followed when he led her to the far side of his truck to block her view of the bloody message alarmed him even more. Although his instincts were to check out her car for any further signs of tampering that could endanger her, Boone temporarily contented himself with scanning the deserted floor of the parking garage over the top of her head.

He reached beneath his jacket to unhook the catch on his holster—just in case—before wrapping his arm back around her shoulders and backing her up to his truck to put another layer of protection between the unseen threat around her. He hadn't seen anybody who'd seemed out of place going in or out of the garage in the three hours he'd been waiting for Kate to get off work. When the shift had changed in the KCPD offices, folks had walked straight in and driven back out. A few might have stopped for a few minutes to chat each other up, but he hadn't seen anybody lingering where they shouldn't be, or sneaking around as if they didn't want to be seen. He'd never even dozed off, but had spent the wait time on his cell, making calls to his brothers and checking in with his deputies back in Grangeport.

Whoever wanted Kate's attention must have done this after the shift change, once her car had been left sitting in the remote corner by itself, facing away from the few vehicles still remaining on this level. Crowded or not, that was pretty brave, walking into a garage used by cops, support staff and legal types, and defacing the car owned by the police psychologist investigating him.

As if he needed any more proof that the man who'd raped and murdered his sister was dangerous.

"Hey." He liked the feel of this woman in his arms, liked the smell of her perfuming every breath, liked the way she held on like she had no intention of letting go—he liked it a lot more than he should for practically being strangers. He hadn't expected the patient, cinched-up, textbook ice princess to be so clingy, so… female. But every cell of his body had been trained to serve and protect. With every beat of his heart he knew that understanding whatever was happening here would lead him one step closer to finding the man who'd murdered Janie. "You keep holding on to me like this, Doc, and I'm going to start to think you like me."

It was a few seconds more before she pulled away without a word. Well, hell, he'd just been teasing, trying to get a smile out of her, trying to get her to talk and clue him in on what seemed to be far more than a tasteless prank. But she was looking at his jacket where she had crushed it in her hand. Maybe the woman was a little shocked. She looked surprised to discover how she'd latched on to him, and equally fascinated by the movements of her fingers, smoothing out the wrinkles in the quilted material, unconsciously petting his chest and triggering a tiny leap of electricity beneath his skin with each gentle stroke of her hand.

"I thought someone was following me. I guess it was you."

"I called out to you when I saw you get on the elevator, but you must not have heard me. I had to circle through every level to find you, but I drove up here as fast as I could."

Boone almost regretted the loss of contact as Kate

stuffed her hands into the pockets of that tightly wrapped coat, and a cool mask slipped over her expression. "You mean you didn't just come up the stairs?"

Her skin was still a little too pale for his liking, but whatever had spooked her—she'd moved past it.

"I was looking for you," he said. "I drove up here, Doc."

"Did you see anyone else? There was a man on the corner—I thought he was going on down the street, but…oh, damn." A fist came out of her pocket and shook the air. "I didn't look at his face. I didn't want to make eye contact and encourage him. How could I be so stupid? What if that was him? What if we just lost our unsub because I was too afraid to look?" She swung her arm out toward the message dripping from her car. "And what does that mean? 'Lies'? What have I lied about?" She wiped at the smear of red on her fingers. Ah, hell. That wasn't paint. "I don't understand. I don't like it when I can't figure out—"

"Take a deep breath, Doc. You're all right."

"No, I'm not. This is all wrong."

Boone gently grasped her by the shoulders and turned her back to face him. He pulled a bandanna from his back pocket and dabbed at the offending mark on her hand. "I didn't see anybody else on this level of the garage. You're safe."

He glanced at the empty space around them one more time, ensuring that was still the case.

But her head trembled back and forth in a subtle *no*. She doubted the sincerity of his words and was getting set to argue some more.

And then, because he'd been in pain all day long, because she'd been rattled by a justifiable scare—because their emotions were too raw and too near the surface to ignore—Boone palmed the back of Kate's neck, dipped his head and pulled her mouth up to his for a kiss.

Her lips parted on a startled gasp. Her warmth rushed to meet him with one breath and hastily retreated with the next. And then a heavy sigh of release relaxed her mouth beneath his and he felt her leaning in ever so slightly. The kiss was hard. It was gentle. It was quick. And even as he savored the hesitant softening and pliant grasp of Kate's lips against his, Boone was pulling away, wondering what the hell had gotten into him.

He stared at Kate for a couple of breathless seconds, taking quick note of the velvety skin at her nape, the artful curve of her pink lips and the thumping of his pulse that charged his body with the desire to kiss her again. Vivid impressions. But none were as clear as the question clouding her verdant eyes.

Why?

Boone pulled his hand from her neck. "You with me now, Doc?" He reasoned away the impulse to kiss her by rationalizing that a peck on the mouth was a far less violent and far more pleasurable way to snap her out of that panic attack than a slap across the face would have been.

Her head moved in the slightest of nods and she pressed the bandanna back into his hands. "If things are safe and no one else is here, there's no need for you to stay—or to—" her fingers wavered in the general vicinity of her mouth "—do that."

"Do *that?*" he echoed. He should apologize for overstepping the boundaries of friendly acquaintances. But Boone wasn't about to start lying to Dr. Kate or to himself. Yeah, he was incensed by everything that had happened today that led up to that impromptu embrace. But he wasn't sorry he'd kissed her. Chances were, however, she was sorry about kissing him back. "Are you okay, Doc?"

She tilted her chin and pasted on a smile. But the white-knuckled grip she still had on her keys didn't fool him. "Thank you for coming to my rescue, but I'm fine."

She was forgetting the badge he wore—and that inexplicable connection forming a bond between them that couldn't be dismissed with a polite thank-you. "We're not going anywhere until you call for backup, have the lab take pictures and analyze that…graffiti, and you file a report."

Kate nodded, dismissing him again. "I'll do that."

Boone stuffed the bandanna back into his pocket, but he wasn't budging.

"Why are you still here, anyway, Sheriff?"

"I realized I never thanked you for everything you've done for me today. I know I didn't give you much of a choice, but you were still mighty gracious about it." The wind whistling through the garage had nothing on the chill Dr. Kate was trying to throw his way. "I figured we both had to eat. Figured maybe you'd let me take you to dinner. To show my appreciation."

"I don't date, Sheriff Harrison."

"Look, about the kiss—I didn't plan that. That's not why I was waiting in the garage for you. I mean, you do eat, don't you?"

"Of course I do. But you don't owe me anything. I was just doing my job today. I don't need any thanks from you. And I certainly don't want to be any more trouble to you. So, good night."

Mules weren't the only stubborn thing his folks had raised on their ranch. Boone pulled back the front of his jacket and splayed his hands at his hips. He didn't get why he was so attracted to this prickly city woman who had to be as wrong for him as his ex-wife had been. But he clearly understood his duty as an officer of the law, and as a man.

"You may not need any thanks, but I don't leave a lady in trouble. I didn't see anyone following you, but that doesn't mean it didn't happen." He inclined his head toward her car. "And clearly someone was here." Easily overriding Kate's protest, Boone slid her purse off her shoulder and handed it to her. "Trust me, kissing you was no trouble. But I promise to keep my hands to myself. Make the call."

"ARE YOU SURE YOU'RE OKAY?" Maggie Wheeler asked, handing Kate a cup of hot tea and sitting beside her on the rear bumper of the ambulance that had been called to the sixth floor of the KCPD parking garage.

"I'm fine," Kate insisted, wrapping her trembling fingers around the warmth of the insulated cup. She appreciated the supportive gesture and true concern from her friend, but hated to see such a big fuss being made over one vandalized car. What she hated more was that the entire task force and several more uniformed officers and a trio of paramedics had shown up in the past hour or so to make a fuss over *her*. "I'm grateful for the tea, Maggie, but don't you think all of this is a little bit of overkill?"

The garage had been deserted an hour ago, but now

it was a beehive of activity. Annie Hermann hovered over the windshield of Kate's car with a flashlight and a cotton swab, verifying that the disturbing message had indeed been written in blood. Pike Taylor's dog Hans had his nose to the concrete, pulling his handler with him along an unseen trail around car tires and concrete pillars toward the elevator. Detectives Montgomery and Fensom had their heads together discussing possible implications of the attack, while two officers unrolled yellow crime scene tape across the top of the stairwell where Pike's dog had stopped to sit and tell his handler that he'd identified a particular scent.

Yet for all the bustle of movement and buzz of conversations, there was one lone figure off by himself, pacing beside the black pickup truck he'd been forced to move to the far side of the garage. Kate's gaze reluctantly drifted over to Boone Harrison's slow, purposeful strides. He was like a hungry mountain lion, waiting for the right moment to pounce on his prey—or perhaps more like a new kid in school who hadn't been invited to join the other students on the playground.

She knew he was anxious to dive into the middle of the investigation, to find answers that would purge his guilt and give him the healing satisfaction of justice for his sister. She understood why he was still here, and was glad that he'd been there to hold on to when she'd been too rattled to think straight. But the man should go home to his family. At the very least, he should go to his comfortable hotel bed and get some much-needed rest instead of wearing a path in the concrete.

And then the pacing stopped and the dark eyes found hers across the distance between them. Kate's fingers tightened around her tea and she huddled inside the blanket the paramedics had draped around her shoulders. What was it about the small-town sheriff that sparked that low hum of electricity inside her and short-circuited her ability to focus on the job at hand?

Her lips burned at the memory of Boone's mouth pressed against hers. Her pulse quickened with the desire to lean against his sturdy chest and feel his solid arms around her again.

She wasn't quite sure why he had kissed her, or why she had stretched up on her tiptoes to kiss him back. There were sound reasons why people in stressful situations turned to each other for comfort and acted out on latent attractions. But she had never given in to such mental weakness before. And she couldn't quite fathom what sort of weakness Boone Harrison possessed that would lead him to such a physical solution to dealing with her panic.

Then Boone turned and his hat shaded his eyes, masking the intensity that she just now realized had left her staring at him like some sort of dumbstruck teenager.

Seriously, Kate? she chided herself, turning her own attention to the tea in her hands and swallowing a mouthful of hot liquid that burned her tongue and knocked some common sense back into her head. *You're too old and too smart to be distracted by a man.* She could ill afford to be blinded by emotions or hormones or whatever it was that made her forget that she'd known Sheriff Harrison for less than twenty-four hours, and that the bulk of that time had been spent arguing with the man or reminding him that he was getting in the way of the work the task force was doing. She'd paid a heavy price for trusting her feelings and believing that the people she cared about had her best interests at heart. She wouldn't make that same mistake again.

While Kate organized her thoughts and evaluated her actions, Maggie continued the conversation. The tall redhead gave a wry laugh beside her. "You should have seen how Detective Montgomery rolled out the cavalry when my ex came after me earlier this year."

Kate inhaled a deep breath that flared her nostrils and gave her time to respond appropriately. "Yes, but your ex-husband had a violent history," Kate argued rationally, suppressing the gut-tightening possibility that someone as abusive as Maggie's late husband had set his sights on her. "There's a big difference between a man trying to kill you and one who just wants to scare you." She nodded toward the detectives at her car. "And that's all our unsub is trying to do—we've rattled his confidence by making some headway in our investigation. He's just reminding us that we haven't identified him yet, and challenging us to step up our efforts to catch him."

Maggie's freckled face creased into a frown. "That's how the violence starts, Kate. With a threat, with intimidation. It doesn't take much more for the fear a stalker instills into every breath you take to become something dangerous or deadly."

A chill that even the hot tea couldn't penetrate shivered through Kate. But she still summoned a brave smile. "I thought you were here to cheer me up."

Maggie dropped an arm around Kate's shoulders and gave her a friendly squeeze. "You're such a strong woman, Kate. I'm sure you'll be fine. But I don't want you to make light of a threat like this. Don't take unnecessary chances. If you feel like someone is after you, and wants to hurt you, let one of us on the task force know. We're going to fight this guy together."

Kate nodded her understanding. "He doesn't get to win."

Maggie smiled again. "Exactly."

"Back it up, pal."

Kate and Maggie both turned at the deep-pitched warning from the parking-garage ramp. Sheriff Harrison had left his truck to stand nose-to-nose with Gabriel Knight, the reporter who covered KCPD's activities for the *Kansas City Journal* newspaper. Only the plastic crime-scene tape and a few inches of attitude separated the two men.

"Oh, no." Kate set her cup down on the ambulance's bumper and let the blanket fall to the concrete at her feet as she hurried over to run interference.

Gabriel Knight was grinning, sarcasm evident in his expression. "Are you the new guard dog on the task force, Sheriff? It *is* sheriff, right?"

Boone didn't bother answering the questions. "That press card hanging around your neck doesn't give you the right to trespass on a crime scene. You might have gotten past the cops downstairs, but you're not getting past me."

"You got in my way this morning, cowboy," the reporter challenged, "but you won't get in my way again. There's a story here."

"Boone." Kate touched his elbow, silently urging him to retreat a step. "I'll handle this." When he straightened his arm to keep her from moving past him, Kate bristled to attention. He was protecting her again. And she didn't need that kind of chivalry right now. "This is *my* job."

He glanced down over the jut of his shoulder at her. "Do you know who messed with your car? Does anyone know? What if it's this guy?"

"Are you accusing me—?"

Boone ignored the reporter's interruption. "I think you'd be a little more cautious about who you let approach you until we get some answers."

"And I think you'd be a little more respectful about departmental protocol." And a little more respectful of the job she'd been trained for. "Creating a scene and alienating the press is not the kind of PR we're looking for."

Gabriel Knight was still looking for his story and the tension between Kate and Boone was feeding right into it. "The grapevine says a task force member received a threat from the Rose Red Rapist. Were you threatened, Dr. Kilpatrick? Is that why Sheriff Cowboy here is so adamant about protecting you?"

Kate turned her frustration on the dark-haired reporter. "Mr. Knight, we're not ready to give a statement yet."

"Is there a problem?" A voice that could be counted on to remain cooler than anyone here entered the conversation. Spencer Montgomery pulled back the front of his suit jacket and splayed his hands at his hips, calmly asserting his authority and making his disapproval of a confrontation on his crime scene clear. "How did you get wind of this threat, Mr. Knight?"

A cocky grin curved the reporter's mouth. "I have my sources."

"If your sources are withholding information key to my investigation—if *you're* withholding information—"

"Can't solve these crimes without my help, Detective?"

Spencer didn't take the bait. "Two things. One—" he took a step toward Knight "—KCPD doesn't talk to you until we're good and ready. So you've got nothing but rumors and hearsay that you can't print. And two?" Kate retreated a step as the red-haired detective turned toward Boone. "Go home, Harrison. I'm glad you were here for Kate. But we've got the investigation covered without your help."

Every muscle in Boone's arm clenched beneath her touch and Kate, not realizing she still held on to him, wisely pulled away.

"You get it right, Montgomery," Boone warned. "All of it." His dark gaze skimmed over Kate, perhaps saying a reluctant goodbye, or maybe just warning her to watch her back, before he met Spencer's icy stare again. "Or I won't care whose jurisdiction it is. I'm finding my sister's killer."

"This isn't right."

He skimmed through Gabriel Knight's article in the *Kansas City Journal* and looked at the black-and-white photo again.

"You're wrong, Dr. Kilpatrick." His breath felt heavy in his chest, making it hard to breathe as he looked at the image of the striking blonde with a dozen microphones and bright lights framing her pale features. "I didn't do the things you said."

He read through the article a third time, and then a fourth. The pungency of the paper's black ink burned his sinuses and stained his hands. The report was extremely well-written. It seemed so plausible, so real.

But it was filled with lies. Kate Kilpatrick and the task force were spreading lies.

Leave it to a woman to ruin his good name again.

He spread the offending article over his desk and smeared away the newsprint beneath his hand. Over and over. And over again until the pressure and friction ripped a hole in the middle of Kate Kilpatrick's earnest expression.

It's not her, a gentle voice inside his head tried to reason. *She doesn't know you. She doesn't know the truth. She can't hurt you.*

Any woman could hurt him if he let her.

No.

"You're damn right, no." He fisted the torn paper in his hand and tossed it into the trash.

And then he saw the black ink on his hands—as vulgar and damning as the red blood he'd washed off his gloves before carefully disposing of them. *She* hated it when he was dirty like this. He hated it.

His chair spun like a tornado behind him as he shot out of it and dashed into the connecting bathroom. He washed his hands and scrubbed beneath his nails three times before he felt the stain of his deeds leave him.

For now.

A knock on the door to the outer room kept him from turning on the water for a fourth time. He dried his hands, then used the towel to open the bathroom door and hurried out to greet his visitor.

"Where have you been? You're late." He verbally pounced on his guest, even before she could shake the water off the umbrella drenched by the thunderstorm raging outside. He watched in horror as dozens of water droplets spotted the carpet.

"It's just water," she said. "Relax."

But he couldn't help the compulsion. He dropped down to his knees and pressed the towel into the rug, soaking up each remnant of rain before the marks became permanent.

He was surprised when she didn't make a joke or grouse about him taking the towel to her wet shoes as well, before she could track any mess farther into the room. *Don't be a fool,* the voice inside his head warned. *She isn't your friend. You can't trust her. You can't trust any woman.*

But the woman knelt beside him, stroked his hair. She laid her hand over his to still his frantic movements. "It's all right," she whispered against his ear. Her loyalty to him was absolute. It had to be. "I know your secrets. I will always keep them for you."

"You'd better," he warned her.

She took the towel from his hands and urged him to his feet. "Go back to work. I'll finish cleaning up."

Chapter Five

"They aren't making any progress, are they, boss?" Flint Larson knocked on the open door behind Boone, announcing his presence before entering Boone's office at the Alton County sheriff's station.

"Not enough to suit me." Boone scrubbed his fingers over the square lines of his smoothly shaved jaw. The midday news broadcast out of Kansas City featured an update on the Rose Red Rapist assaults and murder. Vanessa Owen, the reporter who'd been hassling Dr. Kate outside her KCPD office, filled up most of the screen as she talked about "unsubstantiated leads" and the police being "closemouthed" about the potential witnesses and suspects they were interviewing.

There were uniformed police officers in the background, along with men and women and cameras and heated side discussions. But there was not one mention of the threat that had been made against Kate.

Boone's eyes were fixed on the cool blonde facing the crowd, answering questions from other reporters at a KCPD press conference. Dr. Kate Kilpatrick looked as beautifully sophisticated and composed as he remembered. Her serene facade and articulate words were no doubt a reassuring panacea for a city living in fear. But he was drawn to the darting focus of her moss-colored eyes. The movement was subtle, but he'd seen her furtive glances more than once in the past few minutes. It was as though she was on guard against an off-camera threat.

Did she have reason to be afraid? Had she received another sick message painted in blood? Had there been another type of communication from the Rose Red Rapist? Was there some other man she clung to like a lifeline when her emotions broke through those barriers of self-control and overwhelmed her?

That classy composure had gone right out the window that night in the parking garage. He hadn't had a woman hold on to him that tightly since...hell, he'd never known a woman so desperate to hold on to someone. It was like Dr. Kate had two settings—the I've-got-it-all-under-control ice queen and the passionate, compassionate firebrand that he suspected came out only under such dire circumstances.

Flint leaned a hip against Boone's desk and sat back to watch the end of the broadcast. "Is that the lady you were talking about? The police psychologist who cleared the red tape for you with KCPD?"

"Yep."

"She's been on the news before, talking about the attacks. I can see why they'd put her on camera. She's a looker."

Boone rolled his gaze up to his deputy. "She's the task force's press liaison. And a trained criminal profiler. She knows what she's talking about."

"Maybe she's good. But she's not doing us any favors." Flint arched a golden brow with skepticism. "Has she called you with any updates? Like finding the man who gave Janie that ring you mentioned?"

"Nope. Out of sight, out of mind, I guess."

Although the sweet-smelling psychologist with the cool reserve and passionate grip had never been far from his mind these past few days. Had the woman just been playing him the same way she was working those reporters? Promising phone calls? Keeping him in the loop? Or had that been her assignment the day he'd gone to K.C. to bring his sister home? Do or say whatever it took to get that bullheaded country boy out of KCPD's hair.

If Kate Kilpatrick thought some heavy conversations and a few touches would get rid of him, then she and the entire task force were mistaken. He'd cleared his schedule for a week—and was prepared to take a sabbatical from his duties as sheriff if necessary—in order to get back to the city and track down the answers he needed. If they decided to cooperate with *his* investigation, Boone would allow it. But if they got in the way of finding Janie's killer—or tried to distract him with the good doctor again—then cooperation was off the table.

"Shall we head out?" Flint stood as soon as the news story ended and Boone turned off the TV. "Colt, Shane and Lucas are waiting for you outside."

Hearing his brothers' names reminded Boone of his immediate responsibilities. The four Harrison men had weathered a lot of ups and downs together throughout their lives. Their bond of blood and friendship made them each stronger. They'd need that strength today.

"Is everything ready?" Boone asked.

Flint nodded. "The traffic's been cleared off the courthouse square, and I lined up a couple of the off-duty guys to lead the procession out to the cemetery following the service. I put the word out, too, that everyone was welcome out at the ranch for potluck and reminiscing."

Good. Just how Boone had ordered it for today. After three days of rain had swept through nearly all of Missouri, he'd even gotten the sunny skies he'd wanted for Janie's sake.

There was really only one thing wrong with the way things were running in Grangeport today.

"Come on, boss." Flint put on his hat and headed for the door. "We've got a funeral to go to."

Boone nodded. He checked the gun at his waist, straightened his tie and grabbed his hat off the coatrack beside the door. Then he headed outside to greet the dark-haired man wearing a bolo tie and business suit.

"Colt." He shook his next oldest brother's hand and pulled him in for a hug. As they separated, Boone looked beyond him to the frail woman waiting in a truck beside the curb. "Will Sally be able to make it today?"

Colt's wife had been battling cancer for several months. He turned and winked at the blonde, who blew Boone a kiss. "She's tired, but she's having a pretty good day. She probably won't be able to make the reception, but she insisted on attending the service."

Boone tipped his hat to his sister-in-law. "Good. That would have meant a lot to Janie. It means a lot to me, too."

"I don't think I could get through today without her." Colt's chest heaved with a deep sigh. "I'm not sure how I'm going to get through any day without her."

Boone squeezed his brother's arm. "She's got good doctors, Colt. We'll just keep praying."

"I finally got the rug rats settled down." Shane Harrison, the third-born son of the family, joined them on the sidewalk in front of the sheriff's office. More lawyer than cowboy, the single dad nonetheless wore a Stetson that he pulled off to warn his ten-year-old son back into his truck to keep an eye on his younger sisters. "If they're not being ornery, they're crying. I don't think they've quite grasped that 'Aunt Jane's gone' means they won't see her again."

Boone offered Shane a wry grin. "If you figure out how to explain it to them, then you can explain it to me."

Shane opened his arms to exchange a hug. "That's one answer I don't have. All I want to do is wrap them up in a hug and protect them from days like this."

Lucas, the Harrison clan's youngest brother, strode up to the gathering. "Any word on who's responsible for today yet, Boone?" The tallest and biggest of them, Lucas wrapped each of them in a bear hug. A cop in the nearby college town of Columbia, Missouri, he, too, wore a gun and badge like his oldest brother. "I can't tell you how bad I want to shoot something today."

Assuming the mantle of family leadership as he had since their parents' deaths, Boone tried to calm his youngest brother's temper as well as offer the strength and reassurance they all needed. "I'm working on it, Lucas. KCPD is going to give us answers. We'll see justice done. I guarantee it." He swept his gaze around the strong circle of family. "But today we need to focus on Janie. And on all the friends and loved ones who are going to miss her, too."

"Not a problem," Colt assured him.

"Whatever you say, big brother," Shane agreed.

Lucas made them all smile again. "But tomorrow we kick somebody's butt, right?"

"*I* kick somebody's butt," Boone clarified, giving his youngest brother a teasing swat to the shoulder. "Let's do this. Let's honor Janie."

They each headed to their respective trucks to get the procession to the church started. The service and reception afterward were just formalities to appease their guests.

As far as Boone was concerned, Janie couldn't really be laid to rest until he had the man who'd murdered her behind bars. Or lying in a grave of his own.

SPENCER MONTGOMERY PULLED IN behind the long row of vehicles lining the drive up to Boone Harrison's ranch. "I need you to work your magic on Sheriff Harrison again, Kate."

"My magic?" She'd spent fewer than twenty-four hours with the small-town sheriff, yet in that short time she'd argued with him, reasoned with him, consoled him...and kissed him. Sounded more like out-of-control craziness rather than any kind of magic.

But bless Spencer Montgomery's sensible soul. He hadn't been talking about any male-female vibe she'd felt with Boone. "You've got a way of reading people, even on their worst of days. I need you to put those profiling skills to work and get these people to open up and tell us about the victim."

"Worst of days," she echoed, thinking back to the day she'd buried her husband, and how the day had been as much about painful gossip and feeling like a fool as it had been about grief. She'd been asked a lot of questions that day, too.

"Did you know Brad had a heart condition? That he had a mistress?"

"Do you think she made him take that performance pill?"

"You must be devastated, finding out this way that your husband had been lying to you for months. How do you feel?"

"And she was a good friend?"

"Poor thing. What are you going to do?"

She'd picked up the tattered remains of her heart and pride, grown a lot wiser, and poured herself into her career.

"Has to be done." Spencer turned off the engine and pocketed his keys.

Kate wished she could turn off her concerns as easily. The setting might be different, the tragedy these friends and family would be talking about was different, but a lot of the scene here in the countryside west of Grangeport felt familiar. She glanced around at the groups of people gathered near different cars, the children climbing over a fence and running to a swing set and fort to play. There were elderly women carrying casserole dishes up to the broad front porch that wrapped around the log and stone house where Boone lived.

She spotted him immediately at the top of the porch steps, along with three other similarly dark-haired men she guessed to be younger brothers, shaking hands and trading hugs with the guests attending this reception. The necessary armor that had gotten her through Brad's funeral and the career she'd devoted herself to softened as her heart went out to Boone and his family. "As a counseling psychologist, and not a profiler, I'm rethinking the wisdom of this idea. It looks like the entire population of Grangeport is here. They need time to mourn."

"We don't have the luxury of time with this guy. So far, all our leads have taken us to crackpots and dead ends." Spencer reminded her why they'd driven two and a half hours from Kansas City. "There has to be someone Jane Harrison was close enough to that she shared her secrets—a brother, a friend. The longer it takes us to find out who she was having that affair with, the more time we're giving our rapist to blend back in with society and fall completely off our radar until he strikes again."

Kate nodded, sharing another grim truth. "And now that his violence has escalated to murder, we need to catch him while his nerves are still a little unsettled by what he's done—before he decides he can get an even bigger rush of power from killing his victims."

Spencer adjusted the dark lenses of his sunglasses over his pale eyes and opened the car door. "I don't want our investigation to turn into a search for a serial killer. Been there, done that."

Kate knew the toll that working the Rich Girl Killer case over the last couple of years had taken on the typically unflappable Detective Montgomery. He'd solved the crimes, and a SWAT team had taken out the killer when he'd gone after Spencer's star witness. And while the notoriety of the detective's success on painstakingly difficult investigations like the RGK murders had gotten him the appointment to lead the task force, Kate knew from confidential meetings as counselor and client that there was a lot of damage eating away at the soul beneath his unemotional exterior.

"Me, either." Understanding that victims and their families weren't the only ones who benefitted from a speedy resolution to a crime, Kate unfastened her seat belt. "Let's do this and then leave these people alone to grieve."

Kate tensed at the familiar *ding-dong* of her phone alerting her to an incoming text message. There were a lot of people—clients, coworkers, friends—who might send her a text. But she had three days' worth of reasons she wanted to ignore the summons. But with Detective Montgomery waiting patiently for her to check it, and an unpleasant task waiting to be completed as quickly as possible, Kate inhaled a soft breath and opened her phone.

I'm coming for you, Kate. To silence your lies. You'll never catch me.

Kate's blood chilled in her veins.

"Is that another one from him?" Spencer asked.

He'd seen the vandalism of her car, and the message that had been left for her in some poor cat's blood. The task force was also monitoring the strange reports and vague threats coming in through KCPD's anonymous tip line. The task force knew she'd been contacted via text message by someone they suspected could be the killer. But no one knew how many texts and calls she'd been receiving on her personal phone every time her image appeared on TV or in the newspaper. Annie Hermann's lab had determined the personal calls had come from an untraceable, prepaid cell. Since Kate's name was listed as the public contact person on the task force's investigation, there was no way of knowing if the threats were coming from one person, or if she was being vilified as the scapegoat for frightened citizens who only wanted to feel safe again.

She could relate.

"No." Kate snapped her phone shut and tucked it into her coat pocket.

"Kate." Spencer wasn't buying the lie.

She confirmed his suspicion. "Let's get this over with and find Jane Harrison's killer. Then the threats will stop."

"Sounds like a plan."

Her doubts set aside by the needs of the case, and her fear put on hold behind a smile, Kate opened her door and stepped outside into the crisp, sunny air. As if drawn by a magnet, her gaze sought out Boone again. But the pull of a magnet worked both ways, and an unexpected shiver of awareness danced across her skin when she saw that Boone's eyes were already focused on her. Despite the bustle of activity between them, he'd noticed her arrival.

Had he noticed the fear that made her tremble the way she had that night in the parking garage, too?

Kate hesitated for a moment, snared by the probing depth of his focus on her. She couldn't remember her own husband ever being so attuned to her presence, able to make her feel like she was the most important woman in the room, or—a couple carrying a sleeping toddler walked past, diverting her attention—like she was the only face in a crowd that mattered.

It was a heady, warming—uncomfortable—feeling, considering the day and the details about his sister she needed to share. Secrets had nearly ruined Kate's life.

She couldn't imagine they'd be any easier for Boone and his family to learn about, either.

"Shall we?" Spencer asked, tapping the roof of the car and snagging her attention away from Boone. "I'll keep my distance, since Harrison likes to butt heads. Maybe I can find some local residents who are willing to talk to me. But I need you to talk to the family."

"Of course."

With Kate's first step, the heel of her navy blue pump sank into the mud and sucked the shoe right off her foot. Not a good omen for the success of this visit. But she was nothing if not professional. A little cool mud between her toes and an anonymous threat on her cell phone wouldn't keep her from doing her job—even if she did feel as if she had Fish Out of Water stamped on her forehead. Boone had been the odd man out that day in Kansas City, but it hadn't stopped him from relentlessly pursuing the truth, coming to her rescue and giving her a memorable kiss. With nary a high-rise in sight or a smooth sidewalk to traverse, Kate was far from familiar territory. But she wouldn't let the awkwardness she felt inside keep her from doing right by the woman whose life these people were celebrating here today.

Spencer had joined a gathering of sheriff's deputies, and Kate's shoes were ruined by the time she reached the steps below Boone on the porch. A young deputy with sun-bleached hair nudged Boone and inclined his head toward her. "Boss."

Boone spared a moment to make eye contact and tip the brim of his hat, but he wanted to finish a conversation with the couple in front of him first. "Irene." He leaned in to trade a light hug with the slender brunette. "I'm glad you drove in from St. Louis."

The woman caught Boone's fingers and squeezed them between hers. "I'm so sorry, Boone. I know you and I parted ways some time ago, but Janie was my friend. She was such an outgoing, talented girl. I'll miss her."

Kate watched him extricate his fingers from the woman's grip. "We all will." He reached around her to shake the shorter man's hand. "Fletcher. Thanks for coming."

"I feel like I knew your sister, since Irene talks about your family." He glanced around at Boone's brothers. "There's the muscle, and the brain, and the quiet one. You're the leader. I guess that made your sister the good-lookin' one." The man named Fletcher laughed, but when Boone didn't join in, he sobered up. "I meant that as a compliment. Losing her is a real tragedy."

"Yep." Boone stretched his arm down the steps toward Kate, inviting her to join them. "Dr. Kate? There's someone I want you to meet. This is my ex-wife, Irene, and her husband, Fletcher Mayne."

Awkward was the word of the day as Boone's fingers folded around hers and he pulled her up to his side and dropped his arm behind her, aligning them together as friends, or, perhaps, even a couple. But the introductions had stopped, and the fingers pinching the nip of her waist reminded her of all the well-wishers she'd endured at Brad's funeral. Kate covered the silence by holding out her hand. "I'm Kate Kilpatrick. I'm a... friend of Boone's."

Irene seemed slightly taken aback, but by what, Kate wasn't sure. "Really. You're a doctor?"

Was the woman checking out her clothes?

"She lives in K.C.," Boone added.

The woman's blue eyes widened even further. "Really?" She lifted her blue eyes to her ex. "Boone, you don't like the city." And then it was back to Kate. "You got this big lug off the ranch? How did you two meet?"

Irene's husband reached for Kate with a smooth, buffed and manicured hand. "Forgive my wife's curiosity. I'm Dr. Mayne. But call me Fletcher. I'm a surgeon. And you?"

"Counseling psychologist."

"Nice to meet you." He linked his arm through his wife's and guided her toward the front door. "Come on, Irene. Boone has other guests to talk to."

Once the storm door swung shut behind the exiting couple, Kate scooted away from the faintly possessive stamp of Boone's touch. "What just happened?"

His chest expanded with a deep breath beneath the Western tailored suit coat he wore. "I'll tell you that if you tell me why you're here."

"I need to ask some follow-up questions. Get some personal insight into your sister's life."

Someone jostled against Kate's back and Boone pulled her over to the porch's wood railing, where he sat, putting his warm brown gaze level with hers. "You could have used a phone for that."

Kate's fingertips danced against her palms as she fought the urge to touch the lines of strain that had settled a little more deeply beside his eyes from when she'd last seen him. "If you don't have the answers, I'm guessing someone around here will. It's a little awkward, but the people who can give us the best information about the hometown girl are probably here today."

"Don't you upset anybody."

"I'll do my best not to." She pointed to the front

door where Irene and Fletcher Mayne had gone inside. "And the introduction to the ex? She thinks you and I are an item."

"Let her think it."

"Boone, we hardly know—"

"Fine." He put up his hands, warding off the rest of her friendly reprimand. He tipped his hat back on his head, revealing more of the jet-black sheen of his hair and the extent of the emotional drain these last few days had taken on him. "Let's just say I've about had my fill of making nice and socializing today. I can't fault Irene for maintaining a friendship with my sister." His voice dropped to a husky whisper, and Kate leaned in closer to listen. "But she left me for that man. She didn't want my children, didn't want this place—and finally decided she didn't even want me. And now she shows up with him?" A wry grin creased his rugged features. "Kind of tough on a man's pride, I suppose."

On a woman's, too. Understanding Boone's pain far better than he knew, Kate followed the instincts of her hand and heart. Her thigh brushed against Boone's knee when she reached out to cup his cheek and smooth her fingertips over the grooves beside his eyes. "All of the emotions—hurt, grief, anger, pride—come to the surface at a time like this. No one would think any less of you if you took a few minutes for yourself."

"*I'd* think less of me." Her hand vanished against his face as he covered it with his. He rubbed his warm, sandpapery skin against her ticklish palm, sensitizing every nerve ending where they touched. Just when she thought she needed to say something, do something, move closer or pull away entirely, Boone turned to press a comforting kiss into her palm before pulling her hand down to his lap and lacing his fingers together with hers. He glanced down at her muddy shoes. "Irene was sizing up the mess on your designer clothes. It was a big reason why she left."

It took Kate a split second to move past the unfamiliar liquid warmth seeping from her hand into the rest of her body. When had comfort and understanding turned into something else? "The mud?"

"All the country living that goes with it. You're a lot like her, you know. Sophisticated. Urban." Boone's thumb continued to stroke over her skin, making it difficult to concentrate.

"Is that good or bad?"

"It just is. Sorry about the shoes. We'll talk later, okay? If you'll excuse me, I need to check on my brothers. Make sure they're holding up okay. Food and refreshments are inside." Kate stuffed her hands inside the pockets of her coat to combat the chill as Boone abruptly released her and stood. He adjusted his Stetson squarely on his head and then moved past her to greet an elderly couple coming up the stairs. "Jack. Shirley. Thank you for coming."

And just like that, the unsophisticated country boy without the M.D. behind his name had maneuvered his way out of answering any of Kate's questions regarding the case.

For the moment.

Kate chuckled softly to herself, admiring how slyly Boone had accomplished his goal of getting out of difficult conversations—and he'd done it with a teasing grin, a hushed voice and quick thinking. She had a feeling Irene and the new hubby, who clearly made a lot of money and liked to talk more than he should, had no clue that they'd just been played by a good ol' country boy.

Of course, the frissons of awareness still fluttering beneath her skin were clear evidence that she'd been played, too. But Kate didn't seem to mind as much as she'd expected. Boone had promised her *later*. And for today, for now, at least, she'd believe that promise.

A pair of shoes and a smidgen of trust were tiny sacrifices to make for coming here.

As she grasped the porch railing and surveyed the beehive of activity around her, she knew there were plenty of people here who might have the answers she sought. Kate crossed to the front door and went inside the log cabin house.

She'd start with the two people she'd just met.

"Thanks, Robin." Kate stepped back as Jane Harrison's friend and former employer, Robin Carter, opened her car door. "Have a safe trip back to K.C."

"I will." The floral designer tossed her purse onto the passenger seat, but paused before getting in. "And you'll keep me in the loop if you find out anything about the man who attacked Jane? I told the women who work for me about the safety tips you suggested, but it's still a little scary to be working in that neighborhood. And here I thought it was an exciting, ideal place to open a business."

"It still is. Just keep practicing those safety precautions." Kate had been glad to find someone at the reception she already knew, even if it was just a witness she'd interviewed. "And if you think of any other details about Janie's life these past few months—even something you may have overlooked as insignificant—give me a call."

"I've got your card. Take care."

"You, too." Kate retreated back to the fence as the other woman turned her car around in the gravel drive and headed back to the highway.

She'd learned all kinds of things about Jane Harrison this afternoon. Janie had been a real tomboy growing up. She'd excelled at 4-H and in showing horses, in particular. She'd worked at a diner in town on the square and been elected homecoming queen in high school. She'd studied art at Stephens College in Columbia, Missouri, opened a studio that had failed as soon as the Ozarks tourist season had ended, and had planned a big wedding to the high school quarterback, which she'd called off just a few months before moving to Kansas City.

All interesting stuff—a testament to how well-loved a young woman she'd been. But none of it was helping to narrow down the search for a confidante who could say who Janie had been seeing in K.C. No one here seemed to have any idea about the mystery man in Janie's life.

Turning toward the dramatic beauty of the orange, pink and gold sunset falling behind the dark brown outlines of Boone's family home, Kate sought out the man who'd been avoiding her all afternoon. The crowd in attendance had thinned considerably, lessening Boone's responsibilities as host. And his ex-wife and her second husband had driven away more than an hour ago, making an excuse to depart almost as soon as Kate had brought up the subject of Jane Harrison and her dating life. So there was no reason for Boone to be hiding from anyone.

Unless, of course, it was her.

Maybe the hushed words and sensuous hand holding had been a diversion to keep the conversation from turning to painful subjects. For a few minutes on his front porch, they'd shared an intimate link that, logically, she had no reason to believe. And yet she'd fallen for them—she'd believed that the sheriff had truly needed her for a few moments to recoup his strength, and would seek her out before she had to leave.

Whether she'd been a fool or not, Spencer Montgomery was counting on her to make that connection to Boone again. And with those disturbing threats promising to follow her until this case was closed and Jane Harrison's killer was behind bars, Kate intended to get the job done.

The air was cooling as the sun sank closer to the horizon. Kate pulled the collar of her trench coat up around her neck as she followed the road back to the house where she'd last seen Boone. But a sad sound, a drawn-out breath, a moan of despair, drew her attention to a shiny green pickup truck as she walked past.

As soon as Kate realized she'd stumbled onto Boone's young blond deputy sitting on the rear bumper, looking at a photograph in his wallet and fighting to stem the tears rolling down his cheeks, she raised her hand in an unspoken apology and backed away. But the moment he saw her, he shot to his feet. He snapped the billfold shut and swiped at his eyes with the back of his hand.

"I'm sorry." Kate apologized out loud this time, hating that she'd intruded on the private moment. "I didn't mean to interrupt. I wasn't sure what I'd heard. I was concerned."

"It's all right, ma'am." He gave his face another swipe. "Did you need something?"

The pink tip of his nose gave an indication of how long he'd been crying. She wasn't sure if it was the counselor or the investigator or something else buried deeper inside her that made her take a step closer and ask, "It's Deputy Larson, isn't it?"

"Yes, ma'am. You can call me Flint."

"Are you all right, Flint?"

"I will be. I guess."

She dropped her gaze to the wallet still clutched in his hand. "What were you looking at?"

"Silly for a grown man to cry, huh?" But he rested his forearms on the tailgate of the truck and opened his billfold to a fading photograph.

"It's sillier for him not to care at a time like this." Kate went to stand beside him to look at the picture of a couple at a high-school prom, judging by the matching gown and tux, and corsage the young girl wore on her wrist. The raven-black hair was long and straight, but there was no mistaking Janie Harrison. And the boy was a younger version of Deputy Larson. The high-school quarterback. "You and Janie used to date?"

He nodded. He caressed the photo, then quickly folded his wallet and tucked it into his back pocket as a sniffle hinted at the tears he was suppressing. "We dated in high school."

"I'm sorry for your loss. Today must be hard for you."

Could Flint be the potential link to Janie's past that she'd been looking for?

"I reckon."

A frustratingly brief answer. But Kate had a lot of experience getting people to open up and talk. A direct question relating to a murder was rarely the best way to begin a conversation.

It didn't take long to get an inspiration. She stepped around the scratched-up steel ball of the truck's trailer hitch and ran her fingers along the polished metal die-cut of a rearing stallion that had been mounted over the rear taillight. The reverse image of pawing forelegs and a flying mane covered the opposite taillight.

"Wow. This is some truck." She nodded to the thick, deeply treaded tires that jacked it up higher than a regular pickup. "Looks like you need a stepladder to climb into it."

"No, ma'am." Flint grinned and relaxed a bit. "But the long legs help."

"These decorations are unusual. They look custom-made. Is that the right term?" She looked up at Flint, expecting to see pride in his four-wheel baby. Instead, his nostrils were flaring with emotion again. "Did I say something wrong?"

Flint shook his head. But he smiled before the tears could come. "Janie designed those. She was one of a kind. She was in shop class when the other girls were learning how to cook and sew." He tapped his fist against the customized light cover. "One time I told her that driving this truck made me feel like riding a herd of wild horses, and when my next birthday rolled around, she'd made these."

This pickup was only a few years old. "So you were more than high school sweethearts?"

"I loved that woman. We were together a long time

after graduation. I asked her to marry me. She said yes and made me the happiest man on the planet. But she had her sights set on something out there in the big world. She wanted to be an artist. Somebody famous, I guess." He nodded up toward the house. "Sort of like Irene leaving Boone. She couldn't make her dreams come true here in Grangeport, either."

So it wasn't just the mud Boone's ex had had an aversion to. "What is it that Irene wanted to do?"

"I don't know. From what I hear, she throws parties and raises money for charity. Sounds boring to me. Her doctor came breezing through town one summer on his way to the lake." Flint tilted his head in a conspiratorial nod. "The next thing you knew, they were running away together. Maybe she just wanted to be swept off her feet."

The excitement of a new, illicit relationship had certainly been temptation enough for her husband. No wonder Boone had reached for her and claimed her. At least she would never have to feel the sting of running into a happy ex with the person chosen over her. "Irene cheated on Boone while they were still married?"

Flint nodded. "At least Janie had the heart to end it with me before she left." His gaze drifted off to a distant place and tears glistened in his eyes again. "I thought that was the saddest day of my life. But this…puttin' her in the ground breaks my heart. I always thought that somehow we'd end up together."

She laid her hand over his fist where it rested on the tailgate and gave him a sympathetic pat. The bruises on his knuckles indicated he might have been doing more than crying and looking at photographs as a means of dealing with his grief. "How did you hurt yourself?"

"Punched a wall at the office when I heard the news."

"I'm so sorry." Although a knife of guilt twisted in her gut at taking advantage of the young man's grief, Kate needed more information. "Did the two of you ever talk? After she moved to Kansas City?"

"If she needed a flat tire changed, or wanted to know how to fix a leaky toilet, she'd call." He pulled his hand from beneath hers. "I don't think she wanted her brothers to know she wasn't as independent as she claimed she was."

"She still called you for favors like that?"

"Not lately."

"Because she had another man in Kansas City who'd take care of those things for her?" After a long moment, Flint nodded. "Did she ever say who it was?"

"I never caught a name. It was some guy at school where she taught evening classes. I think she started to feel like the city was home, instead of Grangeport. The phone calls got fewer and farther between." He hooked his thumbs in the belt of his uniform and stepped away with a deep breath. "She didn't need me anymore. I guess she was calling him."

"Doing okay, Flint?" The deep voice from behind Kate explained why the deputy had suddenly straightened to attention.

The young man winked at Kate. "The doc here was listening to my troubles."

"She's good at that." Boone's hand skimmed Kate's back as he moved up beside her. "I know you're scheduled for duty tonight, but if you need some more time, I'll find someone to cover for you."

"That's okay, boss. I'd rather stay busy." He pulled

his keys from his pocket before nodding to them both. "Ma'am. Boss. Hopefully, it won't be a slow night."

"And I always hope that it is." Boone pulled Kate aside until Flint Larson had started his truck and sped off down the road, throwing up plenty of mud onto the clean chassis. "So I'm guessing you're not here to console me. And I know Detective Montgomery isn't." He pointed up to the porch where Spencer stood in a semicircle with Boone's brothers and carried on a conversation. When Kate turned up the driveway to join them, Boone caught her hand and tugged her in a different direction—across the yard toward the barn and other outbuildings. "I've been following the news broadcasts with your reports. Doesn't sound like you've got any leads."

"We're keeping some of our suspicions and information out of the press." She let her hand rest inside his without really holding on. "We still have some follow-up questions we need to ask about your sister, and I think Flint just pointed us in the right direction. Did she ever mention the name of a man at the college where she taught? I think that's the missing boyfriend we're looking for."

He shortened his stride to accommodate the careful steps her high-heels forced her to take across the grass. "You don't think Janie was dating the Rose Red Rapist, do you?"

"No. I don't think so. He's an opportunistic rapist, not a planner. It wouldn't fit his profile." She tightened her grip, telling him without words that she knew these details were difficult for him to hear. "But I do think finding this boyfriend will give us key information about Janie's activities right before she was attacked.

This mystery man may have been the last person to have contact with her. Maybe she said something, or he saw someone…"

His fingers squeezed almost painfully around hers. "What was wrong with this guy that she kept him a secret from me and the rest of us—even from her friends in Kansas City?"

"I think he was married," Kate stated quietly.

Boone shook his head and pulled away. "No. She wouldn't do that. She knows what I went through with Irene. She wouldn't wreck someone else's life."

"She was young and pretty and vibrant, according to everyone I've spoken to here today. What man wouldn't fall in love with her?"

"Falling for her, I get. But Janie having an affair with a married man?"

"Sometimes you can't help who you fall in love with. And he probably lied to her—told her he was leaving his wife, or that they'd grown apart and the marriage wasn't any good." Her own bitterness filtered in. "He's a selfish man, trying to have the best of both worlds— the stability and reputation of a marriage plus the thrill of a conquest."

Kate heard the words tumble out of her mouth and wished she could pull them back when she saw how Boone's gaze narrowed and his lips flattened into a grim line. It was so rare for her to misspeak like that, to utter words without thinking of the consequences, that it shocked her into silence. Had that been Brad's excuse for his affair with Vanessa? He couldn't help who he fell in love with? What lies had he told Vanessa about his marriage to Kate? Had Boone's ex made the same hurtful excuses to him? "I…I'm sorry. I'm sure Janie meant a lot to this man. And I'm sure she didn't mention him to you because she wanted to spare your feelings."

"Unlike you."

She reached for him. "Boone—"

"I'm sorry, too." He backed away, avoiding her outstretched hand. And then he tipped his face to the evening sky and cursed before nailing her with a raw look. "I can't do this right now. Every nerve in my body is fried. Give me an hour to decompress if you want me to think straight." He took a couple of steps toward the barn before looking back over his shoulder at her. "Unless you want to go riding with me?"

Kate's eyes widened. "On a horse?"

For a moment, his expression darkened, intensified. Kate's mind leapt to the idea of riding…other things. Her cheeks felt feverish in the cooling air at the thought of helping Boone assuage his grief with something much more intimate than a conversation.

But if he'd been thinking of a roll in the hay, he never let on. He blinked and the invitation she'd imagined seeing there was gone. "That's generally the way it's done."

She couldn't keep playing these games with him. Barging into her life unannounced. Unexpected kisses. Holding hands, blunt words. He made her say things without thinking and messed up the necessary order of her life. He'd gotten too far into her head already. Way too far.

"If we could just do this now," she begged, "then I could get back to the city, you could get back to your life and we could both get back to work."

He strode away, clicking his tongue against his teeth and calling to a big, tan-colored horse in the corral beside the barn. "I need one hour to myself, Doc. Grange-port isn't that big. I'll find you when I'm done."

"Boone—"

"One hour."

Why was she chasing after him? She forced herself to stop. "Promise?"

He stopped and looked at her then. "Why would I say something if I didn't mean it?"

"Not everyone who makes a promise keeps it."

Kate tilted her chin against the brown-eyed scrutiny.

"I do." He opened the corral gate and grabbed the horse's halter to lead it into the barn. "I'll find you in an hour."

Chapter Six

He didn't have to look hard to find her.

By the time Boone had rubbed down Big Jim and stowed the tack, night had fallen, and the family and guests from Janie's reception had all left. In fact, the only vehicle left in the drive was his own black pickup.

So where was Kate?

Boone ran to the house's mudroom entrance off the kitchen. She'd made such a fuss about him getting back in an hour—okay, so it had been seventy-five minutes—that she'd probably taken off with Spencer Montgomery and gone back to Kansas City. His tardiness was probably all the proof she needed to believe he wasn't a man of his word.

"Kate?" he shouted. Before he'd taken that ride out to the bluffs and back to clear his head and purge the worst of the sadness and rage that had been simmering beneath the surface all day long, she'd seemed desperate that he keep his promise to return to discuss the task force's investigation. And she'd seemed equally certain that he wouldn't. "Kate!"

He tracked his mucky boots straight into the kitchen before he saw her standing at the coffeemaker, pouring a couple of mugs of what smelled like fresh, hot java. The aroma of home-ground beans and the subtler scent of Kate herself filled his nose and drained the fight right out of him.

"You're here." He offered the lame greeting, wondering at the relief coursing through his system.

She picked up one mug and carried it across the kitchen to him. "You said you'd come back to talk."

"I wasn't sure you believed me."

"I wasn't sure I did, either."

Humbled by her honesty, and determined to convince her that she could count on him to do what he promised, Boone took the mug she offered and took a sip of the fragrant, reviving brew. "Thanks."

Relieved to know she hadn't gone and as ready as he was ever going to be to talk about his sister's secret life, he handed the coffee mug back to Kate and took a few minutes to hang up his hat and jacket, and take off his boots back in the mudroom. After securing his gun and badge in a drawer near the back door, he grabbed the broom and swept his trail out of the kitchen. "If my mother was still alive, she'd have a cow over me tracking this mess into her house."

He was curiously pleased to notice that Kate hadn't just made coffee, but had truly made herself at home. She'd kicked off the shoes and hose she'd totaled and was padding around the kitchen in a pair of Boone-sized white socks. When she saw him watching her feet, she thinned her mouth into an apology. "I hope it's okay if I borrow these. I found them folded up in the basket in the laundry room. My toes were cold."

"Not at all." The cotton socks were an odd contrast to the tailored skirt and blouse she still wore, but he liked the homey, not quite so uptight, twist to her wardrobe.

Even something as unsexy as a pair of socks perked up his awareness of Dr. Kate. Could be it was just a little rush of possessive appreciation at the idea of her wearing his clothes. He crossed to the polished oak table where she'd put his mug of coffee. She'd set a place for her mug and cell phone at the opposite end. Just two place settings. Good. "Where's Montgomery?"

She stood at the microwave, watching a plate with a paper towel draped over it spin around. "He went with your brother Lucas to a place called Nettie's for dinner."

"It's a bar up in town that serves sandwiches and appetizers."

The microwave dinged, and she plucked out the steaming paper towel and tossed it into the trash beneath the sink. "I cleaned up a bit and made up a plate of leftovers for you, in case you were hungry, too." She set the plate of casserole samplings on the table and gestured for him to sit. "I know at events like this, the host doesn't usually eat much."

"I didn't. Thanks." He waited for her to sit before he picked up his fork and joined her. She wound her fingers around her mug to warm them while he tasted the cheesy mac and beef and something crunchy with an Oriental tang. He hoped she'd eaten while he was out. He hoped she was ready for the question that had been nagging at him since he'd saddled Big Jim. "So why don't you trust me, Doc?"

"Oh, it's…" green eyes met his across the length of the table, then discovered something fascinating in the depths of her coffee "…it's not you."

Boone took another bite. "So who *do* you trust?"

Her gaze searched the cabinets now. "I don't suppose you have any tea instead of coffee around here, do you?"

"Nobody, huh?"

The mossy-green eyes found him again, conceding trust issues. He had to give the woman credit. Whatever thoughts were running through her head looked like they were pretty tough to sort through. But she wasn't shying away from them.

"Flint told me about your wife—your ex-wife," she amended. "I wanted to apologize for those things I said before at the barn. I know how it feels, when the person you love and have pledged your life to cheats on your marriage. I was letting some of my own feelings get into the mix, and my words wound up being hurtful, and I'm sorry." Irene's infidelity was old news. He appreciated the apology, but hearing some selfish lowlife had treated Kate the same way? Boone stabbed his fork in a meatball and waited to hear the rest. "I, um—the reason Vanessa Owen and I were arguing outside my office, why we don't get along well is—"

"Was she the other woman?"

"Yes. And I felt particularly stupid about the affair because I didn't find out about it—I had no clue—until my husband had a heart attack and died while he was… in bed with her."

"That's rough." Boone forgot the food and reached across table to pry her hand off the coffee she held. He rubbed his thumb over her knuckles, concerned by the chill he felt there despite the warm mug. "I wondered about your husband. You're too smart and too pretty to have never been attached to anyone. He's the stupid one, if you ask me."

"Thanks." She turned her hand in his. "I think the

same way about Irene." Her mouth softened with half a smile. "I spent half an hour talking to her and Fletcher, and somehow the conversation always came around and ended up being about him."

Kate's smile triggered one of his own. "Self-centered jerk."

Tiny lines crinkled beside her eyes when she laughed. "I think Flint was right. She's probably bored out of her mind with that guy."

"I don't know. She said she was bored here, too."

"With that gorgeous sunset I saw tonight? And all the friendly people?"

She'd noticed the sunset? Boone laced his fingers together with hers and studied her expression until her cheeks dotted with color and he was certain her appreciation for the scenery around here was genuine. "Maybe you have less in common with my ex-wife than I gave you credit for."

"Is that a compliment?"

"Definitely."

Despite the blush, an unsmiling gravity returned to her expression. "So, are we okay?"

The glimpse of vulnerability in this normally confident woman touched the places that were raw and hurting inside him. Without releasing her hand, he stood to walk around the table and tug her to her feet. He heard a formal gasp of protest when he palmed either side of her waist and pulled her to him until his thighs could feel the warmth of hers against them. "I want to be more than okay with you, Doc."

She braced her hands in the middle of his chest and leaned back. "Boone—"

"I know you're cautious and guarded and like to

think things through. But right now I just want to feel."
He smoothed the silky, honey-gold bangs off her forehead and pressed a kiss to one golden brow. "I want to forget all I've lost and grab hold of something good."
He watched the caution light go on in those pretty green eyes as he kissed first one cheek and then the other. The pale skin warmed with heat beneath each caress, and the tips of her fingers curled into the muscles of his chest. "I want you to admit that you're feeling what I'm feeling, and find out what good places those feelings can take us to."

He dipped his head and pressed a gentle kiss against her lips. They trembled. Parted. He kissed them again.

"I don't think—"

"Shh." Boone pushed a finger over her lips. "I don't want you to think, Doc. Not about how you've been hurt in the past, not about how you're worried you'll be hurt again. I just want you to feel this moment—be in this moment with me. Trust me. For this moment."

For an endless second, he thought she might not respond to his request. Then she tilted her eyes to his and nodded beneath his hand.

"Not a word," he reminded her. He didn't want logic or fears talking her out of the connection he believed she needed—the same connection he knew he was craving like a thirsty man.

Kate's lips stretched into a smile beneath his fingertip.

With an approving nod and a grateful smile of his own, Boone removed his finger and leaned down to capture her lips. But Kate slid her arms around his neck and rose up on tiptoe to meet him halfway.

Boone's mouth opened greedily over Kate's. She

tilted her face to give him access to every warm corner and soft swell of her lips. He felt the tips of her breasts knotting against his chest as she pulled herself closer. His hands found the sleek arch of her back and the womanly flare of her bottom. He lifted, pulled until he could feel her hips flush against his. He dipped his tongue inside her mouth to taste coffee and heat and the shy welcome of her tongue sliding against his.

The emotions of the day, of the entire week, tumbled together inside him and found an outlet in the white-hot fusion of her lips matching every foray of his, and in the needy grabs of her fingers in his hair, beneath his collar, against his feverish skin.

He had no memory of the ice princess who measured every word and controlled every action. This Kate was open and giving and grasping. She was everything he wanted in a woman, everything he needed. Right now. At this moment.

There were no words, no sounds beyond a gasp for breath or hum of pleasure. There was no thought or reason or doubt. There was only feeling.

The spark of attraction that had been there from their first meeting blazed like a lightning storm between them. And the understanding of two wounded souls coming together in healing passion lit up something close to his heart.

A voice from deep inside his head tried to warn him this was too much, too soon. But the whispering voice was drowned out by pain being assuaged, loneliness being cast aside, trust being nourished and mutual desire being given full rein.

Boone's thighs crowded against Kate's, backing her up against the table as he plundered her mouth. There was zero chill to her fingers now as she unhooked one button, and then another on his shirt to slip her hands inside and brand his skin.

In one fluid movement, Boone lifted her onto the table. If china rattled or silverware danced, he didn't hear it. Blind with need, his fingers found the hem of her skirt and tugged it up her legs. Her thighs were smooth and firm, and opened as willingly as her mouth, welcoming him. Boone pushed impossibly closer between them, nestling his swelling heat against hers.

It was hot. It was passionate. It was perfect.

He hadn't been with a woman for so long. And he couldn't remember ever wanting to be with one as much as he wanted Kate right now. Right here.

A bell rang in head. A mechanical *ding-dong,* like the doorbell, only much, much closer.

"What the...?" Boone dragged his mouth away from Kate's. Who would dare intrude on this moment?

Her breath rushed out in a moist caress against his neck. "Is that...? Where is...?"

He moved his hands to the more neutral location of her back and scanned the kitchen walls and mudroom exit, trying to orient himself to the sound.

"Boone, stop. I need to..." Kate's breathing was as ragged as his own as she pulled her hands from inside his shirt and scooted off the table, forcing him back half a step.

And then he saw light on Kate's cell phone. *1 msg Unknown*

He picked the phone up off the table before she could get turned around. He stepped back to give them each some room to cool off and reclaim some of the sanity he'd encouraged her to abandon. "Got a secret admirer?" he teased.

She snatched the phone from his hand and turned her back on him, putting the width of the kitchen between them. She was straightening her skirt and blouse, fluffing her hair with her fingers, getting that invisible armor into place before she flipped open the phone.

"Isn't it a wrong number?" Everything about her reaction to a misdirected text put him on guard. "Doc?"

"Just a sec."

There was no *just a sec*. The woman was shaking like an autumn leaf on the wind, despite the determined tilt of her chin. And he didn't think it all had to do with the aftershocks of that passionate tête-à-tête that he was still recovering from. Boone crept up behind her on silent feet and peered over her shoulder.

You're not as smart as you think you are, Kate. I will silence you if you don't stop telling lies.

"Son of a bitch."

"Boone!"

He plucked the phone from her hand and read the text a second time. There was no mistaking the threat he read there. Message 10 out of 10. He deflected Kate's hands as she tried to reclaim her phone. Boone scrolled through her Inbox and found seven previous texts from the same unknown caller. Each message was just as cryptic and venomous and vile as the threat she'd just received.

He caught her wrist when she reached for the phone again and held the evidence up to her face. "These are from him, aren't they. The Rose Red Rapist? First he vandalizes your car and now he's stalking you?" He let her pull free and grab the phone from him. "How long has this been going on?"

Her kiss-stained lips and wrinkled skirt warred with the defiance in her eyes. She snapped the phone shut and dropped it into her coat pocket on the back of her chair before facing him. "Every time I appear on television, or I'm quoted in the news—I'll get two or three texts or calls afterward."

"And Montgomery knows about these threats, right? He's putting a stop to them, isn't he?" Boone raked his fingers through his hair as she set that stoic expression into place. "Doc?"

"I'm developing a relationship with him—"

"With a serial rapist?" Anger and fear and misguided bravery were terrific antidotes for the electricity sparking through his system.

He listened in disbelief to the justification for not actively pursuing the threats or throwing away her phone or at least changing her number. "It's key to his profile, I believe. It's a way to smoke him out. He needs to feel superior to strong women—in this case, me. If he fixates on me, then he—"

"He'll rape and murder you, too."

"—won't go after anyone else." Kate's tone grew calmer, more articulate with each ludicrous sentence. She reached up to refasten the buttons of his white shirt and smooth the collar back into place. "He'll expose himself. He'll make a mistake. We can catch him."

That gentle touch, which had tamed his impulsive nature before, barely took the edge off his temper. He closed his fingers around her wrists and pulled them away. "I don't know how Montgomery runs an operation, but here, we do not put innocent people in harm's way for the sake of the investigation."

"Do you want to find Janie's killer?"

"Yes. But I don't want to lose anyone else in the process. I don't even like that you were here at the house by yourself."

Now the ice princess was back. She twisted her wrists from his grip and straightened the cuffs of her blouse. "Fortunately, it's not your call to make, since you're not part of the task force."

She wanted to go there again? He was the one losing the good people in his life. Boone Harrison wasn't about to go down without a fight—be it against a violent killer or the ice-cold logic of a woman whose passion and vulnerability were turning him inside out. "Get your shoes and coat on." He pulled his gun and badge out of the drawer where he'd stashed them and turned toward the mudroom to get his boots. "I'm taking you to Montgomery and we're going to discuss exactly what kind of dangerous mind game you're playing."

KATE DIDN'T KNOW if it was the pinch of her shrunken shoes, the noise from the jukebox and chatter of the bar or the black-haired cowboy arguing every statement she made that was giving her such a splitting headache.

"Let's take this outside," Spencer Montgomery ordered. She doubted that line dancing and country music were the lead detective's taste in evening entertainment, but he seemed to have no problem siding with Boone and reprimanding her about the text messages.

As the small town's sheriff, Boone apparently enjoyed the privilege of parking his truck wherever he wanted, so he'd pulled up onto the sidewalk just outside the front entrance.

As soon as the door to Nettie's closed behind them, there was a blessed reprieve to the decibel level of the noise pounding in Kate's ears. But there was no reprieve in the two-against-one standoff between her and the unlikely alliance of Boone and Spencer.

"How many of these messages have you received?" Spencer asked.

"Eight and counting," Boone answered before she could get a word in.

"Do you mind?" she countered, sensing she'd have a far better chance of reasoning her plan out with Spencer than with Boone.

Especially in the chaotically emotional state he seemed stuck in ever since that make-out session on his kitchen table that she'd foolishly let get out of hand, Kate wasn't so naive to think she'd had no part in how far things had gone. Between his seductive kisses and the hushed confessions they'd shared that had somehow brought them closer, and the bruised ego that truly wanted to believe that a mature, virile man like Boone was into her, she'd let all common sense go out the window. She'd done exactly as he'd asked, turning off the cautious intellect that had saved her from any hurt or humiliation since Brad's death, and simply *felt* the moment.

But she was tired, the headache was throbbing against her skull, and the chance to catch five minutes of quiet time to herself wasn't going to happen here. Maybe Boone could think and function in the midst of emotional turmoil, but she needed to step back and discuss things rationally.

She concentrated on Spencer's cool gray eyes and on the sensible man she knew him to be. "He's contacted me after each of the daily press conferences, and after Gabriel Knight's and Rebecca Cartwright's articles in the *Kansas City Journal*. And there have been two today since this morning's press conference."

Spencer asked to see her cell phone again. "You told me there'd only been a couple of calls. Has there been any physical escalation to these threats beyond the vandalism of your car? Have you had the sense that anyone is following you?"

Did the bullish sheriff pacing behind her count? "No. Only the texts."

The detective scrolled through the eight messages again. "All variations on the same theme. You're sure this is related to the investigation, and isn't something personal?"

"It's damn personal," Boone insisted, stopping at her shoulder.

"But is it a warning to the task force or to Kate specifically?"

She caught her breath at the heat radiating off Boone as he leaned in. "Have *you* gotten any messages that threaten to silence you?"

Spencer handed back her phone and Kate tucked it into the pocket of her coat. "And we're sure the number is untraceable?"

"Annie already checked it out. They're from different disposable cell phones."

"So they could be from more than one person."

"Or from someone who's smarter than you. You need to take her off this investigation, Montgomery," Boone advised. "Or at least put someone else in the public relations spotlight."

"That's exactly what you shouldn't do." Kate flattened her hand in the middle of Boone's unyielding chest and nudged him back a step. "Think about this guy's profile, Spencer. I'm the perfect bait to smoke him out. I'm the enemy he preys on personified. He's made a connection to me before we've been able to nail down a connection to him. If he wants to come after me, then let him."

"Doc!"

She turned to include both men in her argument, feeling a twinge of guilt at the grim lines of strain that had returned to deepen the grooves beside Boone's eyes. "How many women has he already hurt? How many innocent women like your sister have to pay the price for his sickness? It needs to stop." She turned back to her colleague. "People are afraid, Spencer. And I have the means to do something about it. If he fixates on me, he'll break the pattern. He'll make a mistake. Then we can catch the Rose Red Rapist and put him away for good."

"She's crazy," Boone muttered.

"It's a good idea, though." Spencer, at least, could see the merit in taking advantage of the rapist's newfound obsession with her. "From a police procedural perspective."

"Damn good one," Boone agreed.

"Really?" Kate was stunned to hear Boone's support. Or not. "Logically. On paper it may be a good idea." His eyes were unreadable pools of darkness in the shadows cast by the brim of his hat. "Doesn't mean I like it. This guy may never act on these threats. He doesn't confront women—he abducts them in the middle of the night when no one's looking. You can't put her in danger like that."

Kate wanted to reach out to Boone to ease the tension she heard in his tone. But she suspected a reassuring touch wouldn't be welcome right now, so she stuffed her hands into the deep pockets of her coat, instead. "It's not your decision, Boone."

"I know. I'm not a member of the task force. You're not my jurisdiction." His sardonic tone chafed against her ears and made her wish she didn't care quite so much about disappointing him. Or worrying him. Or... just how much did she care about Boone Harrison and what he felt about her?

"She's handled you okay," Spencer pointed out.

"Yeah, but I'm one of the good guys." A tipsy couple came out of the bar and stumbled past them. Boone made eye contact with them long enough to warn them away from the car they were headed to. Only after the man doffed him a salute and the couple walked on down the street instead of driving, did Boone resume the argument. "I have the same goal as your task force—to solve Janie's murder and get this guy off the streets. He's not interested in helping you solve the crimes."

Spencer, at least, was beginning to see the possibilities of the offer she'd made to serve as bait for the Rose Red Rapist. "You'd need twenty-four-hour protection, Kate. And you don't even carry a gun."

"Because I'm not a cop. I only work with them. But I do know how to use a gun."

He nodded. "You'd better start carrying."

She'd need to spend some time on the practice range, too, to refresh her skills. But she'd probably feel safer with her department-issued Glock in her purse, too. "All right."

"Hold on," Boone protested. "You mean you're actually considering this?"

Kate wasn't feeling particularly victorious at the moment. Boone was right. Logically, developing this relationship with the Rose Red Rapist in an effort to draw him out of hiding made good sense. But one woman had already died. Others had suffered terribly at his hands. This was not just a patient she was trying to help to open up and reveal himself. If the threats did become physical, she doubted she'd be able to talk him out of hurting her. Not for long, at any rate.

And could she trust that backup would be there to save her if talking didn't work?

Spencer understood the seriousness of what she was proposing. He wouldn't take advantage of the danger she'd be in just for the sake of solving the case. "We'll have to make at least one protection detail undercover. Too many uniforms around you will drive the unsub off the radar, and you'd be risking your life for nothing."

"She'll have her protection."

Kate tilted her head at the matter-of-fact tone in Boone's voice. He was serious. "I didn't ask you to help with this."

But Spencer seemed to like the idea. "Are you volunteering, cowboy?"

"Wait a minute." Kate wasn't sure who she was arguing with now. "I can't have him around 24/7."

"I thought you two liked each other."

"We do," Boone insisted.

"Makes sense, then. If the two of you are a couple, it wouldn't look out of place to see you together."

Kate's face felt fiery hot. "We're not a couple. He'll get in the way of the investigation. He's…distracting."

"I've never met a more focused woman than you, Kate." Spencer's compliment was meant to encourage her, but her resolve to take on the difficult task of taunting the Rose Red Rapist out of his comfort zone was wilting beneath the conditions being put on her. "Of course, we'll keep pursuing the forensic angle. If we get a lock on this guy's phone or he finds another means of communication we can trace, we'll go after him. But for now I want you to continue following up any leads you have and running the press conferences. Let's put him on the defensive for a change. And someone from the task force, a uniformed officer, or the sheriff here will be watching out for him—"

"And watching over her," Boone added.

"—around the clock." Spencer turned his eyes to Boone. "Can you keep her safe?"

"Yep."

"Then welcome to the team." Spencer shook Boone's hand, then held on to make a point. "Strictly as a consultant. You'll still be out of your jurisdiction, Harrison. So no solo investigation, understood?"

"Understood. I guess I'm heading back to the big city." Boone tipped his hat back on his head, letting the illumination from the streetlamp reveal the promise in his eyes. "Wherever the doc goes, I go."

Chapter Seven

"This is never going to work."

"You can always change your mind," Boone suggested, loosely gripping the steering wheel of his truck as he eased them off the highway into Kansas City's late-night traffic.

"I'm talking about you being here, not the plan."

Kate picked up her purse from the floor of Boone's truck as soon as he turned into the relatively new subdivision where her house was located on the northern edge of the city. She opened the bag and fished for her keys. Getting used to carrying her bag and gun with her everywhere would be an adjustment. Her life seemed to move much more efficiently when she locked up her purse for the day and carried the necessities like keys, lipstick and phone in her pockets.

Once the keys were in hand, she leaned back into the oversize dimensions of the truck's velour seat. "I talk and listen to people all day long. It's emotionally draining. I need some down time at the end of the day— quiet time, alone time. How am I supposed to recover for the next day's work if you're here?"

"You won't even know I'm around."

She rolled her eyes doubtfully and pointed out the next turn.

"I can sleep on the couch or out in my truck if that's the way you want it."

"I do." She thought that offer sounded a little too good to be true.

"But you're not moving from one location to another without me driving you. And if it gets too quiet or I don't have a direct line of sight to you, I'm coming to check it out."

Kate groaned. Since Boone had come into her world just a few short days ago, her life had been more of an emotional roller coaster than anything she'd experienced after Brad's death. She'd carefully reconstructed her daily routine after losing her husband. It was how she coped. "Do you have any idea how much I need my alone time?"

"Who took a ride out into the countryside to get away from it all for an hour or so this evening?" She felt his attention sweep over her before he glanced at the dashboard clock and returned his eyes to the road. "Make that yesterday evening."

The luminous clock said it was nearly two in the morning. And she was feeling every long hour she'd been awake. "But you had the chance to be alone with your horse, or whatever you were doing, and 'decompress,' like you said. How am I supposed to decompress if you're shadowing me all the time?"

"I can teach you how to ride."

Kate snorted at the joke.

"Were you always this much of a control freak, Kate? Or did your husband's cheating do that to you?"

She hugged her purse in front of her, bristling at his questions. "I'm not going to answer that."

"You don't have to." He pulled off his Stetson and dropped it onto the seat between them. Then he scrubbed his fingers along his scalp, indicating that he was feeling the fatigue of the long day, too. "I may not have the Ph.D. after my name, but I can figure people out. You are a passionate, giving, spontaneous woman when you drop the body armor."

"One ill-advised kiss in your kitchen because I let my hormones get away from me—"

"That's what made it so special, so hot. You weren't thinking things through. You were feeling, reacting, trusting your instincts instead of your brain. You wanted me. I wanted you. It was that simple." He pulled up to a stop sign and waited. His eyes were dark and focused and daring her to argue his point when he looked over at her this time. "You may know how to profile people, Doc, but you don't always understand them. Take this crazy idea you've got about 'developing a relationship' with that Rose Red bastard. You're thinking logically. But he isn't. He doesn't care about the plan, and I doubt he'll follow it. He's going to react. Be unpredictable. That's your mistake." He turned his eyes back to the road and pulled out. "Not all of us think things through as carefully as you do, Doc. Don't be fooled into thinking he will."

They rode the rest of the way in silence until Kate pointed out her bungalow. "You can pull into the drive…way."

She grabbed the dash and sat up straight when she saw the garage door standing partway open.

Boone saw it, too. The sudden alertness radiating

off his body and filling up the cab of the truck only increased the uneasy suspicion she felt. "Is it broken?" he asked. "Did you leave it that way?"

"It was closed when Spencer picked me up this morning."

He shifted the truck into Reverse and backed out of the driveway. He drove around the block and pulled up to the house more slowly this time. "Do you recognize the cars around here?"

"It's too dark to see all of them. But of the ones I can make out, yes, they're my neighbors'."

"It may be nothing. The city has had a lot of rain, too, and sometimes all that moisture can mess with the automatic sensors." This time Boone swung around parallel to the curb and parked on the street. Was he anticipating the need to make a quick getaway?

"Wait here a sec." He put his hat back on his head, adjusted the front of his jacket to reveal the official uniform he'd changed into before leaving Grangeport, and pulled his gun from his holster. "I'll check it out."

So he didn't really suspect a faulty sensor in her automatic garage door opener, either. Kate crushed the straps of her purse in her fingers and watched him approach the half-open garage. The only light on the house was over the front porch steps. But there was enough muted light from the nearest streetlamp to see him flatten his back against the siding, tilt his head to listen for sound, and then, with his gun clutched between both hands, duck beneath the hanging door and disappear into the darkness of her garage.

She wasn't aware of holding her breath and counting off the seconds until she reached five. And then her brain finally kicked in over her fear. Boone had gone in there without backup, and the soft leather crushed between her fingers reminded her that her gun was locked up inside the house.

If someone had broken in… If that someone was still there, and he'd found her gun… Boone could be walking into an ambush. An ambush meant for her.

Her purse was on the floor and Kate was out the door. After one step, she stopped to pull off her heels so she wouldn't make any noise on the concrete driveway and walk, and give her approach away. She set one shoe down on the ground and turned the other one around in her fist to use the mud-caked heel as a weapon if necessary.

Kate moved as quickly and silently as she'd seen Boone do, changing course at the last second, thinking that sticking to the light of the front porch would be smarter than following him directly into the unknown darkness of the garage. Ignoring the chill on her bare feet, she crept up the front steps and pulled out the key. She was reaching for the lock when the interior door swung open.

Her startled yelp was punctuated by the storm door smacking into her shoulder. She lost the shoe, lost the keys, lost her balance as a figure dressed in dark colors from head to toe charged out the door and barreled into her.

Kate and the faceless intruder toppled over the edge of the porch and tumbled down together, hitting the edge of every step with a bruising thud.

Dizzy, aching, Kate had the presence of mind to latch on to her attacker, to cushion the crashing fall. When they rolled to a stop, Kate was pinned beneath him. But he wasn't attacking her at all. He was scrambling to his knees, struggling to get away.

"I'm with KCPD. Stop. Boone!" Kate shrieked, grabbing on to a gray hood, a dark brown sleeve, whatever she could reach to hold the perp in place. Adrenaline gave her strength, but freedom motivated her squirming opponent. With his legs straddling her waist, he sat up, jerking the edge of the stocking mask from her fingers to keep his face covered. Kate pushed up on one elbow, desperate to hold on to and identify the intruder, their suspect…the Rose Red… "Boone—!"

A wicked right cross slammed into Kate's face, knocking her to the ground. She'd been struck by something hard and square, a tool rather than a fist. Her cheek split open, burned. Her vision blurred. Her grip weakened and the dark figure slipped away.

Without a threat, without a word—without any attempt to harm her beyond his desire to escape—he left her and ran through her neighbor's yard and disappeared into the murky shadows.

"Kate?" The storm door slammed again. She heard Boone's boots on the stairs.

She rolled over onto her hands and knees and pushed herself up. "There." She pointed to the neighbor's yard. Dark brown coveralls. A hooded face. "That way." She wobbled. "Go!"

The images tried to match up with a memory. Another day. Another attack. She had a brief vision of long legs giving chase. But her balance was a pendulum swinging back and forth inside her head, and she finally gave up on the idea of standing and collapsed onto her burning cheek.

"Kate!" In a matter of seconds, she felt herself being

turned, lifted. And then she was leaning against the solid warmth of Boone's chest. "Doc?"

He was down on the ground with her, cradling her in his lap. Her pillow rippled with muscles and crisp cotton beneath her cheek as Boone holstered his weapon, pulled out his phone to call 911, and wadded up his handkerchief to dab at her wound.

She winced at the sharp pain that stabbed through her entire skull. "It was him. Did he get away?"

"I let him go."

"We had him. The man from the parking garage."

He easily overpowered her protesting hand and pressed the white handkerchief against her cheekbone again. "Honey, you're bleeding. Did you hit your head? Are you hurt anywhere else?" She rode the heavy, frustrated breath that expanded his chest. "What part of 'stay put' don't you understand?"

When he wouldn't ease up on the pressure on her cheek, Kate held on to his wrist to pull herself into a more upright position. The dizziness was subsiding, and the need to prove that she hadn't just done a completely idiotic thing was growing. "My gun is in the house. If I called out to warn you, he would have known you were there. He could have shot you."

"He could have shot *you*." Kate realized that she still had something from her wrestle on the front walk clutched in her fist. Pushing Boone's fingers aside, she took over holding the stained handkerchief against the cut on her cheek and let him adjust his hold to help her sit completely upright. "Uh-oh. I'm learning that look. Doc, what are you thinking?"

"That man was dressed just like the guy I saw outside the parking garage at work last week. The one I thought was following me. But I got a piece of him this time." She held up the black knit glove she'd pulled off her assailant. "This glove would almost fit me. He has small hands."

Boone peered around at the trees and houses and vehicles again, either ensuring the perp hadn't returned or looking for the backup he'd called. "What little glimpse I got of him, he wasn't that tall. Maybe that's why he hits his victims from behind when he abducts them." She used him as a brace to sit up on her knees, and he moved to kneel in front of her. "Did the guy who tackled you seem strong enough to haul a woman in and out of a van?"

"Strong enough, I suppose. He surprised me as much as anything. I'm sure he got a little beat up and disoriented on the trip down the steps, too, so that's probably why I could pull this off him." She held up the glove. "We need to get this into evidence in case there's DNA on it. And we need to call dispatch with a description of his clothes—brown coveralls, gray hoodie, stocking mask—no wonder I couldn't see his face that day."

"I'll call it in, I promise. But we need to get you inside and get that cut cleaned up. If it's bleeding too badly, I'm taking you to the E.R." He pushed to his feet, holding out his hand to her. "Can you get up?"

She folded her hand into his, but paused before standing. She could see the bloodstain on the front of his jacket now. Her blood. His clean white handkerchief was streaked with crimson. No wonder he'd been so concerned and given up his pursuit. She must look even worse than she felt.

Misreading her hesitation, Boone pulled her to her

feet and swung her up into his arms. He caught her behind her shoulders and knees and carried her up the steps.

She pushed against the wall of his chest. "I'm not a damsel in distress. I can walk."

"Well, I'm an old-fashioned kind of guy, so let me do this." She *had* given him a good scare. She could see it in the tight lines in the beard stubble bracketing his mouth. If a little old-fashioned chivalry would ease his concern and keep him amenable to her strategy to catch the rapist, then she'd give herself permission to relax against his strength and heat, and feel a little bit like Snow White being rescued by Prince Charming. Once he'd opened the door and carried her into the foyer, he halted. "Do you have a first-aid kit?"

He didn't set her down. Kate pointed down the hallway. "In the bathroom off the master suite."

But when he carried her through the door to her bedroom, her fingers curled into his chest and the fairy tale ended. Boone set her down, pulled her behind him and put his hand on his gun.

Kate buried her face against his shoulder. "Okay. Now I'm distressed."

"I'm calling Montgomery directly." He turned to gather her in his arms and walk her away from the utter destruction of her most private sanctuary.

But the images had been instantly and indelibly etched on her brain. Slashed pillows and drapes. Broken mirrors and picture glass. Roses scattered all over her bed. And one word, painted in red, on the wall above her headboard.

Silence!

Boone rubbed at the fatigue burning his eyes. The pulsating lights of the ambulance and police cars in Kate's driveway and lining the street in front of her house didn't help the lack of sleep that was pulling at his body. They didn't do much to ease his concern that there was nothing any of these people could do to keep Dr. Kate safe from the bastard who had already killed his sister, either.

A dozen uniformed officers swarmed around the place while he stood on the front walk listening to members of the task force discuss the break-in and the intruder who was probably already home getting some shut-eye.

He understood the intricacies of a long-term investigation, and the patience required to evaluate every possible lead, dismiss worthless intel and decide which pieces of evidence or witness testimony required even more evaluation. But while Spencer Montgomery and the others gave their reports, Boone's attention kept shifting over to the stubborn, barefoot blonde sitting on the ambulance's back bumper. The paramedic tended to the wound on Kate's cheek and checked for other minor injuries while the tall redhead in the KCPD uniform, Sgt. Maggie Wheeler, who was apparently a good friend as well as a coworker, took her statement and kept her company.

For a few brief moments, Kate's eyes locked on to his and the weariness inside him eased a bit. He'd been scared that she'd gotten hurt—sick to think, even for a moment, that he'd failed to protect her the same way he'd failed Janie. A couple of butterfly bandages and an ice pack for the bump on her head, and Kate claimed she was okay. But should a reassuring smile from a woman who'd complicated his life in so many ways in such a short time really have such a profound effect on him?

Normally, Boone wasn't one to question his instincts when it came to people and investigations and doing his job. The one place he'd ever misjudged something important, the one time his instincts had been wrong, had been his marriage to Irene. He'd loved her hard, believing she wanted the same things he wanted—roots, children, a long life together. But once the magic of the honeymoon had worn off and the real work of making a marriage strong had set in, she'd grown more distant. She often had a reason for working late in town, or a business trip to take. She'd secretly stayed on birth control while he'd believed they were working on starting that family. In hindsight, he was glad they hadn't created a child in a marriage that had been falling apart. But he'd thought Irene was the one for him. It had been a tough blow to his pride and his heart to realize that he was only *the one for now* with her.

Now here he was, getting tangled up hard and fast with Kate Kilpatrick. She was a city sophisticate with a Ph.D. who wore sexy, impractical shoes and knew beans about horses—not too unlike Irene. But she had a big, compassionate heart beneath that chilly exterior. She was intellectual in ways he couldn't always fathom but had to admire. And she had to be about the sexiest woman he'd ever put his hands on, especially when he got the idea that those clutching fingers and fiery kisses only worked on him.

Should he be listening to what his instincts were telling him about Dr. Kate? Or should he take a cue from the good doctor herself and spend a little more time thinking things through before he let her into his heart any further?

A whiff of panting wet dog at his feet drew Boone's attention back to the gathering of KCPD task force members.

Pike Taylor, the big cop who'd kept him from crossing the crime scene tape to see where Janie's body had been found that first day he'd come to Kansas City, tossed a knotted toy to his German shepherd companion to reward him for doing the job he'd been trained for. "Hans followed the perp's trail until it went cold. He lost the scent about a quarter mile down on the next street over. I'm guessing the perp got into a vehicle and drove away at that point." He knelt down to play a little tug-of-war with the big dog. "I did a little house-to-house work, too. Nobody we talked to remembered seeing any vehicles they couldn't identify. One guy said he thought he heard an 'expensive' engine gunning out on the street that woke him. But at this time of night, most of them were asleep, so no one saw anything. I gave them Dr. Kilpatrick's description of the intruder and warned them to keep their eyes open and their doors locked. Call us if they see anything. The usual spiel."

Boone shook his head. "This guy was only after Kate. They're all safe."

"Try telling them that." Pike pushed to his feet and glanced around, indicating the lights coming on in nearby homes and shades opening for the curious and the frightened to peek out.

"He's right." Kate brushed her hand against Boone's elbow and he stepped to one side, letting her and Maggie Wheeler join the conversation. "We need to turn off these flashing lights and get some of these vehicles out of here, Spencer, or we're going to cause a panic. And I'm sure the press will get wind of it before the sun comes up, if they aren't already on their way here."

"I'll take care of it, sir," Pike volunteered. "I need to get Hans a drink of water, anyway." He called to another uniformed officer, standing guard beside the yellow crime scene tape marking off Kate's front steps. "Yo, Estes. Come give me a hand."

The young, dark-haired officer hurried over, then jumped back half a step when he startled Pike's dog. The big German shepherd spun around, baring his teeth. Pike shouted one word and the dog dropped to his haunches, then crawled forward to a down position, although his nose stayed in the air sniffing something on the wind.

"He probably smells my girlfriend's dachshund on me." Officer Estes lowered his hands from the surrender position and tucked his thumbs into his belt as soon as Hans gave up his interest in him and Pike Taylor led him away to his departmental SUV. He smiled at Kate like they were old friends. "Dr. Kilpatrick, are you all right?"

"I'll be fine, Pete. Thanks for asking. And thanks for helping out tonight."

"Glad to do it, ma'am." Boone noticed the twenty-something standing up a little straighter under Kate's praise. Then he glanced around the group, clapped his leather gloves together and scooted off after the K-9 cop and his dog. "I'd better get going. What do you need, Taylor?"

Was Boone overreacting to be suspicious of Pete Estes? The dog didn't seem to like him. But that hardly made him a suspect. There were a couple of things, like motive, means and opportunity, to be considered first. After tonight's events, he supposed he'd be paranoid about any man he didn't know addressing Kate.

The others in the circle appeared less concerned. And the kid was doing his job. The ambulance and two of the squad cars pulled away while Detective Montgomery turned to Annie Hermann. "What about the message on the wall?"

The petite CSI cringed as she peeled off her gloves and stuffed them into the pockets of her navy jacket. "Maybe I'm what set Hans off. It looks like more cat blood, but I'll have the lab run it to make sure. I wonder if we should start talking to animal shelters, see if anyone has reported a missing pet. It makes me sick to my stomach to think of how much blood volume it would take to leave these messages."

"Cat lover?" Nick Fensom teased.

She glared at the burly detective. "I've rescued a couple. The messages and vandalism are bad enough. But when I think of the cruelty behind them… Our unsub clearly has no conscience—no qualms about hurting anyone or anything."

Nick patted the petite woman on the shoulder. "I'm sure your tabbies are safe, Hermann."

"They're Siamese." She tucked several unruly dark curls behind her ears and excused herself. "I need to get that glove and these samples back to the lab."

"Can't say anything nice to that woman," Nick groused.

"You need to make an appointment with me sometime," Kate gently chided him. "We can work on those communication skills."

Boone slid his hand behind Kate's back, battling the

urge to wrap his arms around her to shield her from the chaos around them. "Fix him later, Doc. We need to get you out of the open here. Get you someplace safe."

Spencer agreed. "Let's wrap this up. Was there anything taken from the house?"

Boone tried to speed the process along. "I secured her gun. It's in my truck. But this break-in wasn't a burglary. Nothing like a TV or sound system was taken. As for anything personal? Don't make her go back in there and look."

Kate slipped away from Boone's touch and crossed to the yellow tape. "It's okay. Maggie? Do you mind coming with me? We can do a quick sweep. I'd like to get some shoes and a change of clothes before my feet freeze, anyway."

Boone could feel the walls already going back up between him and Kate. Maybe his instincts about her were as off as they'd been about Estes, and that this need burning inside him was all one-sided. Maybe the protective—possessive—turbulence of his emotions was just the result of Dr. Kate being the person who'd been there when he'd needed someone to connect to.

Didn't make it any easier to concentrate on work, though.

Once the two women entered the house, Spencer turned to Boone. "Anything else you can tell us?"

"The perp I chased was a small guy. I'm six foot and he was at least a couple of inches shorter."

Nick Fensom straightened up beside him. "My height?"

"Maybe. But not as muscular." Nick was built like a Mack truck. The man Boone had chased from the house was more of a sports car. "And like Kate said, the guy had small hands."

Spencer jotted the details in his notebook. "Five-ten, wiry build. We'll add that to the description."

"So what about Kate?" Was Montgomery even considering what could have happened tonight if she'd walked in on the guy slashing up her room with a box cutter or small knife? "You're giving up this crazy idea about using her as bait, right? I mean, this guy has found her car, her house—now he's put his hands on her."

The detective tucked his notepad inside his suit jacket. "I offered to move her to a safe house, but she insisted on a hotel room with periodic drive-bys to watch over her for now. I don't think you're going to get her off this case."

Kate herself had something to say about that. "You won't. I'm still your chief profiler and press liaison. I don't want to be locked away where this guy can't reach me at all. I still want to put the Rose Red Rapist away for good."

She came down the stairs with another pair of those sexy high heels she favored on her feet and an overnight bag hooked over her shoulder. If Boone overlooked the two butterfly bandages and puffy bruise forming beneath her left eye, then she was looking the part of the consummate professional again. But he did see the cut and bruising, and with her hands buried in the pockets of that dusty, smudged-up trench coat—hiding the telltale indicators of her true state of mind—he couldn't tell how much of the confident facade was real, and how much of it was a cover for tight fists or trembling fingers.

"But I do need a hot bath, a good night's sleep and some time to myself to think through a theory I have."

The facade was convincing enough for Detective Montgomery. "What theory?" he asked.

"Wait until the next task force briefing. I need to work it out with a clear head first. But it could change the focus of our investigation."

"I look forward to it."

Boone tossed Kate's bag in the back of the truck and cranked up the heat, giving the cab a few minutes to warm up before he drove to the hotel where Maggie Wheeler had made arrangements for Kate to stay. She still had her hands hidden inside her pockets and had leaned back against the headrest and closed her eyes.

He didn't even turn on the radio for company as he waited, thinking she'd nodded off. But a minute later, she surprised him. "I don't think I've been this tired since going through the emotional wringer of Brad's death. I didn't sleep much then, either."

"Avoiding your emotions is how you keep your energy up?"

She opened her eyes and lolled her head to the left to face him. "It's a defense mechanism and you know it, Dr. Harrison."

He grinned at the reference to his earlier claim that he didn't need a Ph.D. to understand people's behavior. "Personally, I think you use up less energy if you just go with the flow of what you're feeling instead of trying to reason out all the potential consequences."

"That can be your dissertation topic when you decide to become a full-fledged behavioral psychologist."

Boone's grin became a chuckle. The woman's clever sense of humor revealed she was a lot tougher than she looked. "So, since we're talking hypotheses…" she giggled at the big word coming out of his mouth "…what's this new theory you have about the Rose Red Rapist?"

Her smile faded and she turned her focus back out to the men and women still working the scene in front of her house. But talking was what she did for a living, and she was willing to share. "I've been thinking this for a while—that this stalking bit doesn't fit the profile of our unsub. Our rapist is a cockroach who doesn't want to be seen. Who is so good at not being seen, in fact, that, after all these years, we have virtually no description of him. I've seen the man in the brown coveralls twice now. A stalker wants someone to know he's there. And after my run-in with that guy tonight… I think we're looking for two unsubs. The rapist and—"

"—a copycat who identifies with him?"

"At least a fan who thinks he's helping him."

As horrible as the thought of having two whack-jobs out there was, Boone could see the logic of her idea. "The guy in your house tonight—the stalker—he may even think he's protecting his…hero…from KCPD, the task force and the face of that task force. You."

Kate nodded. "Me. I'm thinking this unsub is younger. He's following all the publicity of the case, and might see Rose Red as a role model. He has the compulsion to hurt women, to terrorize them—but he hasn't progressed to the stage of attacking them."

Boone's hands tightened on the steering wheel. "What about tonight? He attacked you."

"That was a fight-or-flight reflex. He wasn't expecting to find me there. He just wanted to get away and I was in his path." She faced him again. "He heard or saw the big, scary cowboy coming into the house after him, and ran out the opposite direction."

"And plowed into you."

She reached up to touch the mark on her cheek. "What do you think he hit me with? It wasn't a gun. Or a knife."

"From the pattern of the damage done in your bedroom, CSI Hermann thinks he was armed with a box cutter." Boone stretched his arm across seat to brush her soft golden hair away from the injury. "You're damn lucky you didn't lose one of those beautiful eyes."

He felt her skin warming beneath his touch and leaned across the seat to kiss her. But a firm hand in the middle of his chest stopped him from getting too close. "Not here." She dropped her hand and glanced out the windows. "Not where the others can see us."

"I think they've already got an idea about us, Doc." Boone pulled his hand away, turned on the headlights and shifted the truck into gear. "I'm just not sure you've got the same idea."

His foot was still on the brake when she slipped her hand out of her pocket again. He could see the little tremors in her fingertips as it slid across the seat toward him, out of sight from all the cops and coworkers and curious onlookers outside. Maybe she did have some inkling of that idea.

Boone reached out, swallowed up her hand in his and held on tight.

She offered.

He accepted.

His instincts were telling him to hold on to this woman any way he could. He likened this uncertain relationship to taming a stubborn, ill-used filly. The desire to work with him was there. But it would require patience and practice and building an unshakable trust before she could truly be his.

Now he just had to make sure a raping killer and his blossoming protégé gave them the time he needed to make that happen.

Chapter Eight

The last of the bubbles had popped and gone by the time Kate decided she'd soaked long enough in the hotel room's spacious bathtub. She reluctantly opened her eyes and forced her jelly-soft muscles to wake up so she could unstop the drain and climb out.

She wrapped a warm towel around her middle and crossed to the mirror to run a comb through her hair and fluff the short strands into place. She could wash her hair and relax the tension from her body with a steamy bath, but there was no toning down the evidence of going head-to-head with the intruder who'd broken into her house. Leaning over the sink to get a closer look, Kate gently touched the sickle-shaped cut beneath her eye. Her cheek wasn't as swollen as it felt, but she'd be wearing a natural blue, purple and violet blush for a while.

Every bruise on her body stood out against her pale, freshly washed skin. The chill that shimmied down her spine and raised goose bumps across her arms and legs could be attributed to the variations in temperature between the bath water and the air, but she suspected her sudden inability to feel warm had a lot to do with being up for nearly twenty-four hours, and suddenly, fully, realizing just how close a call she'd had.

Whether she'd confronted the Rose Red Rapist or a wannabe sidekick, her injuries could have been so much worse. She might be lying in the morgue like Janie Harrison had, instead of lying in a hotel bathtub until every cell of her body had finally relaxed. Unable to shake the chill, Kate pulled one of the fluffy white terry robes off the back of the door and wrapped it around her body, towel and all. She tied the sash around her waist and opened the bathroom door.

"It's as rejuvenating as a long ride on a good horse, isn't it." Boone Harrison was stretched out on the sofa in the suite's sitting area, with his feet propped on the coffee table in front of him. His voice sounded drowsy in the room's dimly lit shadows. But Kate had a sense of unblinking eyes focused squarely on hers, as if he'd been watching the closed door the entire time she'd been in there.

Feeling her temperature rising again beneath those warm brown eyes, Kate knotted the robe a second time, wondering if it was possible for him to tell that she'd left her pajamas in her bag in the suite's separate bedroom. "Well, the scenery may not be as striking, but I bet it's a lot easier on the muscles."

Boone rose from the couch and strolled across the room. "Depends on what scenery you're looking at."

He lifted the collar of her robe and pulled it to the base of her throat, covering the top of the towel and stretch of skin she'd inadvertently exposed across her chest.

All the blood seemed to rush to Kate's face as she plucked the collar from his fingers and clasped it together at her neck. His suggestive compliment and teasing smile warmed her in ways a bath and robe could not. Good grief. She was almost forty and blushing like a schoolgirl. Time to check her hormones and remember why they were sharing this hotel suite in the first place.

She moved toward the clock on the coffee table before consciously remembering to breathe again. "It's five in the morning. Do you need help unfolding the sofa bed out here?"

"I got it covered, Doc. I set out the spare pillows and blanket, pulled all the blinds in both rooms—for security's sake, as well as keeping the sun out when it comes up. I verified that one of Montgomery's squad cars has circled the place at least twice. And the Do Not Disturb sign is on the door."

"You've been busy."

He grinned. "You were in there a long time."

She returned his smile, then changed direction toward the bedroom door. "We have permission to sleep in as long as we need before the task force debriefs, but I think we'd better say good night."

If Boone had picked up on the raw nervous energy she felt, he was either too tired or too polite to call her on it. "Everything's locked up tight so you can get some rest, Doc. I still want to jump into the shower if you've left me any hot water."

"A little." She wasn't such a schoolgirl around a mature, virile man that she couldn't throw out a little teasing, too—or appreciate that his presence here *did* make her feel safe. Saf*er,* at any rate. "I'm doing the right thing, aren't I? Drawing this guy out so we can catch him?"

She could tell he still wasn't completely sold on her

theories about the case. "If that bastard or his sick little sidekick shows his face, I will take him out before they can hurt you. I promise you that."

It was a promise she desperately wanted to believe. "Good night, Boone."

"Good night, Kate."

Weary and wrung out both physically and emotionally, Kate changed into her pajamas and crawled under the covers. She'd barely turned off the light and rolled over before falling into a deep, hard sleep.

Exhaustion claimed her body.

But her mind couldn't seem to shut down and let her rest.

From the darkest shadows of dream land she heard laughter. Not teasing. Not funny.

Painful laughter. It was a man's and a woman's voices, mocking her. Wounding her.

Kate thrashed in the bed, fighting to wake herself before the nightmare could claim her. But she wasn't strong enough to spare herself.

"You think you're so smart." Vanessa Owen wandered out of one dark corner of the hotel room as horrid dreams came to life. She walked hand in hand with Kate's husband, Brad. "You have no clue about men and women and the world, Kate. They don't need you. They'll leave you behind."

Brad was dressed in the tuxedo he'd worn on their wedding day. The gold ring she'd given him glinted with an unearthly green light. "So smart," he laughed. "So stupid. We all leave."

They walked up to the bed and circled around her. Laughing. Pointing. Kissing. Forcing her to watch their happiness while the bed beneath her turned mucky, spongy like black quicksand.

"Stop. Don't do this." Kate argued with the haunting images to make them disappear. They leaned over her, pushed her down, surrounded her in the black hole that sucked her down into the murky abyss. She reached for her husband. *"I love you."*

"Not good enough, Kate." His laughter deepened, filled up her ears.

"You said you loved me." She caught hold of his hand, but she was sinking. Drowning. *"You gave me your word."*

"I lied." He let go of her hand and she plummeted into the darkness.

"Stop." Kate clawed her way to the surface. She struggled to wake herself, to find her way back to the real world of light and hope. *"Stop it!"*

"So, so smart." Vanessa leaned over her. Her long, curling hair dangled in Kate's face, caught in Kate's mouth and choked her. *"So, so stupid."*

"Stop." Kate tried to brush it away, to speak, to pro-test—to beg if she must. But her arms were trapped, her body pinned.

The corners of the room swirled with shadows, cir-cling around, closing in. Other hands were on her now, dragging her down. Squeezing the air from her lungs. Stopping up her mouth. Crushing her throat.

She tried to scream, but the unseen hands wielded slashing silver blades. They cut her tongue, sliced her throat.

Stop.

Laughter.

Stop.

Darkness.
Stop.
Silence.
"Stop!"

Kate flung herself out of the grasping pit of darkness. The scream tore through her and she startled herself awake.

She clutched at her neck and opened her eyes, unsure what was reality and what was nightmare. She was still in her hotel room. There were still dark corners. Still shadows.

There was one tall, dark, broad shadow, in particular—throwing open the door to stand silhouetted against the light from the other room.

"Doc?"

KATE KICKED OFF THE COVERS that had wound around her body and scrambled onto her knees and across the bed to flip on the lamp.

The small circle of light chased away the darkest of the images that terrorized her. It also gave shape and form to the figure standing in the open doorway.

"Boone?"

"Yeah, Doc, it's me."

His gaze swept around the room. He opened the closet door, checked behind each curtain, then crossed to the bed. Details registered now that the shadows were fading. He carried his gun pointed down at his side. His damp hair glistened like polished onyx, run through with shards of silver. His hastily buttoned jeans rode low on his hips, as if he'd jumped out of bed and run in here, expecting to find an intruder.

The only intruders had been the cruel images conjured by her emotions. Kate's hands fisted at her throat and stomach. She was still breathing hard and deep, and her heart thudded against her ribs.

"I was having a nightmare."

"You think?"

Her gaze dropped briefly to the gun. But the rock-steady gaze and piercing alertness of the man standing above her compelled her to tip her chin up to face him. She pulled the covers into her lap. "I woke you. I'm sorry."

"At least I know you've got a good scream in case you really are in danger."

She knew she was meant to laugh, but couldn't quite summon the sound from her throat. Boone tucked the gun into the back of his jeans and sat on the edge of the bed. He pulled her hands off the covers and rubbed them between his palms. "God, woman, you're like ice. I heard you cry out and came to check. I thought your friend found a way to scale the building and break through a locked window to get to you."

She watched his hands and felt the magic effect they had on her. So rough in texture, so gentle in touch, his big hands were sheltering, soothing—and shared an abundant warmth her nightmare had stolen from her.

"I'm afraid the only danger is inside my head." She squeezed her eyes shut against the gritty sensation of gathering tears. "I think too much, don't I? And then an idea gets stuck in my head and I'm too stubborn to believe any differently." She blinked her eyes open and the evidence of all her frustration, fears and fatigue spilled over. "I can never just leave well enough alone."

"Hey, none of that. You'll get your bandages wet." He caught the first tear with the tip of his finger and wiped it away. He patiently caught another, and another, until she sniffed and regained a dubious control over her emotions. "You want to talk about it?"

She wiped away the next few tears herself and sniffed again. "I'm the counselor. I'm supposed to help other people talk about things."

Boone got up to stack the pillows against the headboard, straighten the covers and tuck them securely around her. The bed shifted when he sat back down on top of the duvet beside her. He leaned back against the pillows and pulled her into his arms, nestling her injured cheek against the firm heat of his chest.

"You talk to *me*," he ordered on a velvety-toned whisper.

The armor surrounding Kate's heart cracked open, without any hope of repairing the protective barrier this time. Without thinking, she wound her arm around his waist, found damp, warm skin to hold on to, and leaned into his strength and comfort.

For several minutes, he simply held her in silence. Kate's head cleared as she drank in the spicy, fresh scent of his skin. She pulled strength from him and felt his abundant heat slowly working its way through her body. The shelter of Boone Harrison's arms chased away the threat from the shadows and her imagination.

Trusting that he meant what he said about listening, she began to open up and share a little about the nightmare, and the realities that triggered it. She talked about her marriage and Brad's affair with Vanessa—how the relationship and people expert had felt like a failure—clueless, betrayed, heartbroken. She talked about rebuilding her life and focusing on her career, how she felt a special affinity for female victims of violent crimes and often did pro bono work helping them find their voice and confidence again. She talked about the things she'd seen the Rose Red Rapist do to a woman, and how driven she felt to get him off the streets so those victims could stand a chance of emotional recovery.

Every fear, every compulsion, had woven its way into her nightmare. The emotions, the personal threats. She'd wanted to fight, to defeat those demons. But she'd been helpless, powerless, a victim herself all over again.

Boone's fingers stroked the hair at her temple. His steady breathing and strong heartbeat evened out the tempo of her own. And he listened. Just as he'd promised. He listened.

"...and I couldn't talk. They humiliated me and hurt me and kept me from speaking. I just wanted somebody to listen."

"I wouldn't worry about that dream." His fingers paused their gentle massage.

"No?"

"Honey, once you get an idea in your head, nobody's ever going to shut you up."

With that, Kate did laugh. She was ready to now. They both laughed. She felt close to another human being. And all was right in her world. For now.

And then another kind of closeness filled the hushed intimacy of the room. Boone tunneled his fingers into her hair, cradling her nape and the side of her jaw as he tipped her head back and kissed her. Kate anchored her hand at his shoulder and held on as he gently, tenderly, explored and reassured. She welcomed him into her mouth, tasting the minty bite of his toothpaste, savoring the catlike rasp of his tongue sliding against hers.

She slid her fingers up into the coal-black silk of his hair and pulled herself more fully into his leisurely, thorough embrace. He kindled an ember of heat deep in her belly, and it spread into every limb, into every cell, until every inch of her, from the tips of her breasts to her once-frozen toes, was on fire.

"Kate." Just as her brain was shutting down and her body's craving to crawl right into his heat was taking over, Boone rolled away.

But he pulled away from the needy clutch of her fingers for only a few moments. He reached behind him and then she heard the heavy thump of his gun being set aside on the nightstand. "Boone?"

"Dr. Kate." He came back to her, scooting down on the bed and quickly reclaiming her mouth as if he'd missed the hungry pressure of their lips joining together as much as she had. He slipped his arm beneath her and palmed her butt. He squeezed and lifted, dragging her to lie more fully on top of him, bunching the covers between them. And as her body softened against the teasing hints of hardness beneath the layers of cotton and batting, Boone shifted the intensity of his kisses into something far more seductive than sharing strength or comfort.

His hands slipped beneath the hem of her long-sleeved tee and the elastic waist of her flannel pants. Every callused stroke against her skin made her want the same freedom to explore the textures of his body. She tugged in frustration at the covers until she could lay her palm over the swell of a flexing pectoral. The muscle quivered beneath her touch. The flat male nipple tightened and poked between her fingers. The crisp dusting of dark hair tickled her sensitive palms.

"Sweet Dr. Kate." His raspy beard stubble grazed along her jaw and the soft underside of her chin as he followed the path of her pulse with his lips and tongue.

Kate arched her neck and then her back, granting him access to every needy nerve ending that longed for his touch. He pulled her up along his body, the shifting covers and friction between them revealing the evidence of his desire.

She snatched at the covers between them, wanting to feel skin on skin. His fingers tugged with a needy lack of finesse, finally pulling her shirt off over her head. Before she could free her arms and toss it onto the floor, his lips reached up and caught her breast in his mouth. She gasped in pleasure at the swirl of his tongue against the pebbled tip and collapsed against his mouth, stabbing her fingers into his hair and clutching his scalp, urging him to deepen the sensual torment of his rough beard and soothing tongue against her most sensitive skin.

And then he was sliding her pants down her thighs, sitting up and spilling her into his lap, reaching between them to unhook the lone button holding his jeans together.

But when she felt the bulge in his jeans pulsing against her, Kate knew a split second of painful inadequacy. She flattened her hand against his chest and pushed. "Wait. Boone, stop."

His chest heaved beneath her hand, and his voice was a ragged gasp. "Did I hurt something?" His eyes were clear, probing, as he captured her face between his hands and brushed his thumb near the bruise on her cheek. "I know you took a pretty hard tumble."

"No, I..." She pulled her hands back to cover her body. "I wanted..."

He bowed his head in a frustrated sigh and rested his forehead against hers. "Ah, Doc. We're going to think this through, aren't we?"

"We've been through a lot in the last few days. We've spent time together, and..." Leaving one arm covering her bare breasts, she latched on to his wrist and tilted her gaze up to his, begging him to understand that this hesitation was all on her. "You may have expectations of me that I can't deliver."

"Honey, I'm not going to force you."

"I know. You would never do that. And God knows you've got the goods..." Kate shrank back from his gaze and felt her entire body heat with embarrassment. "Please tell me I didn't say that out loud."

His worried expression stretched into a Boone-sized grin. "Maybe I shouldn't worry about how much you like to talk. That may just be the best damn compliment I've ever had. And trust me, Doc, the feeling is mutual."

She tilted her eyes to him again. His flattery was wonderful, as much of a stroke to her fragile feminine ego as the proof of his words still evident beneath the covers. But he had to see the logic in what she might be sparing him. "Thank you, but...you have needs, and I—"

Boone swore. He said words she hadn't used in a long time, and he said them twice. "That lowlife bastard scum of an ex didn't deserve you."

The grip he held on her face strengthened, yet somehow gentled at the same time. "When was the last time you were with a man? It was with him, right? And what, he probably stopped sleeping with you and blamed it on too much work or not understanding his needs—and all the time he was screwing someone else?"

Kate read the turbulence in his eyes. She felt it in the shaking control of his fingertips. Had he gone through something similar with his ex-wife? Had Irene ever made this utterly masculine and virile man feel like anything less than he was?

Kate nodded. "Something like that."

He kissed her square on the mouth. "He's not a part of your life anymore, Kate. I am. It feels right. I want this. I want you. I haven't wanted any woman for I don't know how long until I met you. You're in my head day and night. I want to feel those sexy hands all over me."

His vehement argument was making sense. Sort of. "My hands are sexy?"

"What you do with them is." Brad had called her beautiful. A lovely compliment, easy to say. But Boone talked specifics. Striking scenery. Pretty eyes. Sexy hands. "Do you believe me? Please, Kate. I need to know that you believe how much I want you."

She nodded, believing.

"And I need you to believe how much I think you want me, too."

"I do want you. I want this."

His grip on her eased. The smile crept back across his features. "I want you to be completely sure."

Kate dropped her hands to the covers between them. She matched his smile and stretched up to kiss him. "Do you have a condom?"

Leaving time for nothing but feeling, nothing but wanting, nothing but trusting that this was right, Boone fell back against the pillows and pulled Kate with him. In a flurry of bumping hands and laughter, of climbing out of bed and diving back in again, they slipped off clothes and stole kisses and burned away any lingering shadows from the past.

Soon, there were no covers, no clothes, no doubts between them. There was only Boone. Rising over her, sliding inside her, claiming her mouth with the same exquisite thoroughness with which he claimed her body.

Kate clutched his hips between her knees to welcome him more fully. She slipped one hand down between them and touched her fingertips to where they were joined. Boone moaned at the brush of her fingers and his entire body went taut.

"Oh, Doc," he panted against her ear. "Damn sexy."

He thrust one more time, carrying Kate over the edge with him as he poured out inside her.

She hugged him close as his body went slack and he collapsed beside her. They dozed in each other's arms for a few minutes, until the sheet cooled and goose bumps shivered across her skin.

Boone pulled the covers over her and left her for a few minutes. But after she heard the water run in the bathroom, he came back and slipped beneath the covers with her.

He gathered her back into his arms and she studied her ordinary, unadorned hand resting at the center of his chest. "Sexy hands, hmm?"

"Oh, yeah." He splayed his fingers over hers and trapped them against the reliable rhythm of his heart.

She'd opened herself up to Boone this morning, baring far more than her body—sharing more with him than she'd shared with any man, including her late husband. She felt raw inside—curiously content, but emotionally wrung out. She recognized an important breakthrough just as she would recognize one in a client. But she also knew that a mental and emotional catharsis didn't mean she was instantly cured. She had scars on her heart that would still require time and nurturing in order to heal.

But for the first time since she'd learned of her husband's infidelity and death, Kate believed that she *would* heal.

She rested her cheek against the pillow of Boone's shoulder. "Would you stay for a little while? At least until I fall asleep?"

He pressed a kiss to the crown of her hair. "You're not gettin' rid of me."

With that promise to hold on to, she smiled and drifted into a deep, dreamless sleep. She knew she was safe from the demons in her imagination as well as the real ones out there in the world—for now.

She'd take for now with Sheriff Boone Harrison.

She'd trust…for now.

Chapter Nine

"He's not our man," Boone muttered under his breath. He closed the door behind the graduate student who scooted past him into the hallway outside the Fairfax Community College art room and turned to face the older man who'd replaced the student at the makeshift interview table across from Kate.

"Professor Ludvenko?" Kate asked.

Boone took a half step back into the room until a sharp glance from Spencer Montgomery reminded him that he wasn't officially a part of the investigative process here. Biting down on his frustration, Boone anchored himself in his boots and did what he'd silently been told to. *Stay back and watch the door. Make sure this stays a private conversation.*

Door duty? Really? He'd been in the police business at least as long as Kate, and certainly longer than Spencer Montgomery. And now he was stuck watching through glass doors and windows into an empty hallway while Kate and Montgomery interviewed every male on campus who'd had any sort of regular contact with Janie.

This was their fourth interview this afternoon. If this Maksim Ludvenko was the guy she'd been seeing, then Boone really had lost touch with his sister these past few months. The long-haired weasel with the eastern European accent was as far from anyone Janie had ever dated in Grangeport as a chicken was from a horse. He'd much prefer hearing that Janie had been dating that younger graduate student, or the nearsighted academic adviser they'd talked to before that, than this guy. Surely this man was too old for his sister. The fact that the fiftyish art professor would rather pick at paint stains on the table where he sat across from Kate than look her in the eye when she asked a question didn't sit well with him.

Professor Ludvenko was too fidgety, too evasive to not be guilty of something. The more Kate prodded, the more he dodged her questions and protested as though he was the victim. That self-preserving egoism didn't sit well with Boone, either.

"Professor Ludvenko, please." Kate pulled a folder from her purse and opened it on the table between them, displaying far more patience than Boone could have mustered. "We're just asking for information about your colleague. We're not accusing you of anything."

Boone didn't know how Kate could sit there and coolly ask Maksim Ludvenko questions about the classes he taught at the Fairfax Community College, when he wanted to put his hands around the guy's throat and ask him point-blank if he'd had an affair with Janie that had ended so badly, he'd killed her. Or maybe he'd ask if raping strong, independent women was more his style.

"I cannot talk about this here." Ludvenko waved a dismissive hand in the air and glanced up at the red-haired detective circling behind him, ostensibly glancing at the half-finished canvases mounted on easels throughout the room. "Not with this man watching over me or that man there, his eyes accusing me of things I did not do."

Boone nodded at the professor, glad to be included in the conversation, and happy that the man could accurately read his thoughts.

"Then just talk to me," Kate reasoned. "Ignore them. Did you have a personal relationship with Jane Harrison?"

There was no trace of either the mind-blowing passion or the vulnerability she'd shown him early this morning in their hotel room. Dr. Kate Kilpatrick couldn't be ruffled by a lack of proper sleep, a late-night attack by a crazed fan or spending several hours sharing her most personal fears and desires with him. Maybe she could turn her emotions on and off like that, or maybe their time together hadn't affected her as profoundly as it had him. He was falling in love with Dr. Kate. Hook, line and sinker. It would be kind of nice to think she was feeling more than empathy or had the hots for him.

That doubt of hers must be contagious, because this morning he'd been certain the falling-in-love stuff was mutual. And now the ice princess was even harder than usual to read.

But then, maybe the cool, calm and collected act was for Ludvenko's benefit. The professor shot up out of his chair and headed for the bay of windows opening into the hall. "I cannot talk about this now. My wife is teaching accounting upstairs—"

Boone blocked his exit out the door. "Sit down and answer the lady's questions."

"No. I want my attorney."

Montgomery flanked the artist on the opposite side. "You don't think your wife's going to know something's going on then?"

"Sheriff, Detective—it's all right." Kate walked up to the professor and tapped his arm, urging him to face her. "Just have your attorney meet you at the Fourth Precinct offices. We'll take you in and do the questioning there."

"Oh, yes," Ludvenko snapped sarcastically. "That would be so much better." Classes must be changing. All of a sudden the handful of students meandering through the hallway were now thirty or forty people walking past. Ludvenko looked through the windows, catching the eyes of a few curious onlookers. Perhaps he decided getting this over with as quickly as possible was a better choice than climbing into a police car out front and setting all sorts of tongues wagging. "Fine. I will answer your question." He made a sharp reverse turn and returned to his seat at the art table. "I do not date my students."

"Janie wasn't a student. She taught jewelry making and welding sculpture classes. She was a colleague of yours…and your wife's." Kate unhooked the button of the blazer she wore and sat. "Maybe we should ask the other Professor Ludvenko if she knew who Jane Harrison was seeing."

"Fine. Yes. I was sleeping with Jane. But I am not this monster you speak of—this rapist." He waved his hand in the air again. "I did not do the things you are accusing me of."

Detective Montgomery resumed his nonchalant stroll through the forest of easels. "If you think the Rose Red

Rapist is a monster, then help us out. Tell us everything you can about Miss Harrison. The more we know about the night she was attacked, the better we'll be able to narrow down the time frame of the assault. If we know more about her state of mind, about who she talked to that night, about who she saw—then it can put us that much closer to finding her killer."

Boone was developing some grudging respect for the unflappable detective. He was as calm and logical as Kate. On paper, they'd make a perfect match. Sophisticated appearances. Scary smart. Cool under pressure.

While he was…hell. He'd better *watch the door* and keep an eye on the students in the hallway to stop anyone from coming in.

"Janie and I were kindred spirits. She possessed the soul of an artist—like me." So Ludvenko was the creep who'd taken advantage of Janie's big heart and thirst for life. "My wife, she is all about numbers and calculations—a good match for any man. But Janie…she was passion."

Boone was getting irritated. "So your wife holds down a steady job, keeps a good home and enjoys a respectable reputation in the community."

"Yes, my wife is all those things."

"In other words, she's boring."

"Boone," Kate cautioned.

"Harrison," Montgomery warned.

"Yes…no." Ludvenko turned his argument away from Boone and pointed across the table at Kate. "Dorothy is a good wife. Do not trick me into saying things. I will deny them all in court."

Kate seemed pleased to finally have his full attention. "But you and Janie shared common interests—your love for art and learning? A passion for life?"

"Yes. We were drawn together at an artists' retreat we both attended one weekend. We continued to see each other when my wife traveled or worked late, whenever we could."

Man, wasn't this scenario sounding familiar. The roles were reversed, of course, but it wasn't too unlike the excuse Irene had given for straying from their marriage.

"Did you see Jane Harrison last Friday night?" Montgomery asked. "I already checked at the business office—your wife went to Phoenix for a weekend symposium."

"No. She did not." Ludvenko grew defensive at the detective's interruption. "She was scheduled to leave, yes, but Dorothy came down with a cold. Her sinuses were so bad that flying was out of the question." His manic gesticulations had been reduced to picking at paint on the table again. "So I called Janie and canceled our weekend getaway. She was not pleased. And then I read in the paper that she was murdered."

Detective Montgomery had a follow-up question. "And your wife will confirm that you were home with her all night?"

"Yes." He pounded his fist against the table. "I lose the woman I love, and I cannot even grieve for her... because of my wife."

Sarcasm poured through Boone's blood. "I'm crying for you, pal."

"You do not understand what we felt for each other."

"Better than you know. I pity your wife."

When Ludvenko turned back to the relative safety

of addressing Kate, she pointed to the picture of the ruby-and-diamond ring she'd set on the table. "Did you give this to Janie?"

"Yes. For her birthday." His mouth curled with a rueful smile. "She said it would be a better present if I were to leave my wife and we could see each other without hiding from the world."

"You never had any intention of leaving your wife, did you?" Boone accused. "You had your cake and were eating it, too."

"I cannot help what the heart feels." He threaded his fingers through his lion's mane of hair. "I know she deserved better. But I would never hurt Janie. Never."

Kate tapped the photo again. "Did she like this ring? It doesn't exactly seem her style." Where was she going with these questions about the ring?

"It was expensive. It proved my love to her."

Boone snorted.

Both Kate and Montgomery glared him into silence again.

While Kate folded the photo into the file and sat back in her chair, pondering some unknown question, Detective Montgomery walked up beside Ludvenko. "Did she contact you at all that Friday night? Or early Saturday morning? The phone records we downloaded from her cell phone show she called a local motel—the Highway 40 Inn. Maybe she was hoping you'd changed your mind?"

"I told you I stayed home with my wife. Janie did not call me after I canceled. Like I said, she was very angry. Besides, we would not stay at a cheap motel. I treated her better than that. It was always the Muhlbach downtown. We liked…the historic architecture."

Montgomery pulled his cell phone off his belt and walked away. "The discretion of a doorman and an old-monied hotel didn't hurt, either, I'm guessing."

"One last question, Professor Ludvenko." Kate stood and gestured around at all the projects on display in the room. "Are any of these paintings Janie's?"

"No. As you said, she was a sculptor. She liked working with metals." He pointed to an oxidized copper sunburst hanging behind his desk. "That is her work."

The interview was over, and though Professor Scumbag alibied out for the night of Janie's rape and murder, Boone decided the man was still guilty—of feeding his sister false hopes and breaking her heart. Crimes he hoped Dorothy Ludvenko would make him pay for with a good divorce attorney.

"So who was Janie calling at the Highway 40 Inn?" Boone asked, once they were outside in the crisp sunshine.

Spencer Montgomery was still on the phone as they walked to Boone's truck and his car. "I'll get the motel to fax over a guest list for that night." He paused before climbing in behind the wheel. "Kate, are you up for the daily press briefing?"

"I am." She answered with more confidence than Boone had expected for a woman whose car and home had been vandalized, and who still bore the vicious bruise of her stalker's last attack where there was no hiding it from the cameras. Not to mention the fact that one of those reporters she'd be facing had wrecked her marriage. He wondered if the confidence was real, or a show for the senior officer on her team.

"Get her back to the office in one piece, Sheriff," Montgomery ordered.

"You got it."

Boone opened the truck door for Kate, then got in behind the wheel and started the engine. The ice princess was a little less icy now that Montgomery had driven away. She was studying the photos in the evidence file again, and her mouth was twisted in a perplexed frown. And while he admired her toughness, wisdom and patience as a profiler and interrogator, he was incredibly drawn to this softer, more pensive version of Dr. Kate.

He waited until she tucked the file back into her purse to throw the truck into Reverse and back out of the parking space. If she wasn't going to share whatever was on her mind, then he'd start the conversation. "So we found out Janie's big secret. She *was* having an affair with a married man. And after the way Irene ended our marriage, Janie probably thought she couldn't talk to me about it."

Kate's focus came back from the wheels spinning inside her head. "She may have thought that being the other woman would have hurt you. I get the idea that she didn't want to be a disappointment to her big brother."

Boone shifted the truck into Drive. "She was my baby sister. I loved her. We'd have worked it out."

"Maybe she thought that she was a grown-up now—not a baby anything—and that she should resolve the problem herself."

"That independence got her killed," he muttered with a mix of guilt and frustration. "And we're no closer to finding out who did it."

"You haven't let her down, Boone." The woman sitting across that seat really *could* read people.

He reached over to squeeze her hand. "It sure feels

like it." Grateful for her insight and compassion and how her gentle reassurances soothed him, Boone returned his grip to the wheel and pulled onto the street. "Ludvenko's not our man. Even if his wife hadn't vouched for his whereabouts last weekend, frankly, I don't think he's smart enough to be the Rose Red Rapist. He's too self-absorbed to feel threatened by any woman, and with that temper of his, he'd have made a mistake by now. Left a clue at one of his crime scenes."

"I agree. He's not the Rose Red Rapist. Or Janie's killer."

He glanced across the seat to see those moss-colored eyes waiting for him to ask, "You still think we've got two different unsubs?"

"No." Boone didn't see it coming. "I think we've got three."

"Is it true you were attacked by the Rose Red Rapist, Dr. Kilpatrick?"

Kate blinked through the spotlights and camera flashes to focus on Vanessa Owen, standing in the front row of the KCPD press conference. A dozen or so reporters, their sound and camera crews, concerned citizens from the community and a cadre of plainclothes and uniformed police officers maintaining some degree of order in the Fourth Precinct's first-floor lobby, crushed forward at the sensationalist question.

She wasn't above letting the disdain for her onetime friend show on her face. But she put up her hand to quiet the buzz of speculation and follow-up questions. If nothing else, it was her job here today to calm their fears, and thus the city's, by not allowing rumors and misinformation to be splashed across headlines and television screens.

Only when the noise had quieted down to a few clicks and whirrs of equipment running, did she speak.

"I was *not* assaulted by the Rose Red Rapist." She articulated the announcement as clearly and succinctly as the human voice would allow. "Despite the drama your colleague Ms. Owen would like to capitalize on here today, there have been no reported rapes in the Kansas City area this past week."

Gabriel Knight wasn't about to be outscooped by Vanessa. The newspaper reporter raised his pen for permission to speak. "So what did happen to you?"

Kate pointed to the cut and angry bruise that was too obvious for even makeup to hide under this many lights. "My home was broken into and I sustained an injury trying to prevent the intruder's escape."

"What did the intruder take?" Gabriel asked.

My peace of mind? The idea that I can be safe alone in my own house, among my own things? Out loud, Kate shrugged off the question with a smile. "Nothing."

"There wasn't a threat? There wasn't a warning, about the task force getting too close to making a breakthrough on their investigation? Kate? Kate!"

She ignored Vanessa's questions for now. If the woman wanted to let the past be forgotten and work together as professional women, then by damn, she could speak to her as a professional, and not rely on either the personal connection they'd once shared to earn her any special privileges, or that arrogant sexuality that up until a few days ago had made Kate feel somehow inadequate and inferior to intimidate her.

Vanessa Owen may have once been an emotional

thorn in Kate's side, but now she was just a reporter. Like anyone else in this room, she was no threat to her. No one here, except for the broad-shouldered sheriff with the warm brown eyes that scanned the crowd and occasionally met her gaze to offer silent encouragement, had the ability to get under Kate's skin and mess with her emotional equilibrium.

"Dr. Kilpatrick?" Finally, the dark-haired reporter figured out the snub. There might even have been a note of newfound respect shading her eyes when she asked her next question. "Was there any sort of threat directed toward you from the man who broke into your home?"

"Yes," she answered honestly, earning another buzz of follow-up questions and photographs. "But again, I do not believe the message came from the Rose Red Rapist. KCPD investigates any number of crimes, from simple vandalism to something as heinous as rape and murder."

Gabriel Knight jotted something in his notepad. "So you're telling us that members of the task force have been threatened by someone besides their target?"

Kate swallowed hard, maintaining her composure. "I'm telling you that *my* home was broken into. No one else's. And that KCPD is investigating the break-in. Don't print anything in your paper that isn't true, Mr. Knight."

The dark-haired man winked. "Rest assured, I always check my facts, Doctor."

Kate went on to reiterate the task force's working description of the Rose Red Rapist, compiled after his assault back in May, and on the Janie Harrison attack. They were looking for a young to middle-aged man with access to buildings undergoing remodeling or new construction, someone with long-standing ties to the community who had the ability to move in and out of different neighborhoods and social situations without drawing attention to himself. "Our unsub is in good shape physically, and probably very fastidious about his appearance and his actions."

"That's it?" Vanessa asked. "Another listing of the profile? I suppose you want us to just keep talking about the neighborhood where he abducted his last two victims and murdered a woman last week?"

Did Kate dare mention her theories about the different unsubs? Would she be giving the frightened people of Kansas City a false sense of hope and security if she told them that she didn't believe the serial rapist they were all terrified of hadn't killed anyone?

If anyone besides Vanessa had asked, she might have mentioned it. But Vanessa was goading her into feeling defensive again and revealing more than she should. Kate stuffed her hands into the pockets of the green tweed blazer she wore and waited for the reactive instinct to pass.

A subtle movement from the corner of her eye diverted her attention. Boone was closing in to warn Vanessa to ease up or shut up or get lost or worse. The subtly protective move warmed her, reminded her of his promise to take care of her. But the reminder that she wasn't alone against pushy reporters or anyone else reminded Kate that she could take care of herself. With a shake of her head, she told Boone she was all right and was able to handle the taunt.

A theory was one thing. Proof was another.

It was in the best interests of the department and of

the city itself to withhold information now rather than
to retract it later.

It was in Kate's best interest to deal with Vanessa
herself and not have to rely on anyone else, not even
Boone, to shield her from dealing with difficult people
and awkward situations. "I believe it's helpful to your
viewers and readers to have the description and safety
precautions repeated." She looked straight into the lens
of the camera next to Vanessa. "We will solve this case.
We will find this man. We're learning more about him
every day. But until that time, we must all be vigilant
and protect ourselves. Don't give him the opportunity
to strike again. Thank you."

Having covered all the talking points required of her,
Kate walked away from the podium and wove her way
through the crowd toward the bank of elevators, despite
the barrage of questions that followed her.

"What new things are you learning, Dr. Kilpatrick?"

"If you don't know who broke into your home, how
do you know it's not related to your investigation?"

"Are you in danger, Doctor?"

"Are you afraid?"

An unseen arm jostled against Kate.

"I'd be afraid," a hushed voice warned.

She spun around, expecting to see a face attached
to that threat. But the flash of a camera blinded her. A
very real hand closed around her arm.

Terror fired through her veins and burst out in a
frightened gasp. Instinctively, she plunged her hand
inside her bag and reached for the gun holstered there.

But another hand, one bigger and rougher than hers,
closed over the unseen man's wrist and freed her.

"Go," Boone ordered beside her ear. The wrist he'd

grabbed twisted free and disappeared with its owner into the crowd.

Kate snatched at a handful of Boone's borrowed KCPD jacket and pulled herself up onto her toes, trying to see into the shifting crowd. "That was him."

Him who? Her stalker? A serial rapist? Someone else?

"Boone? Did you see—?"

"Go." He snugged his hands around her waist and pushed her to the edge of the crowd. "You need to get out of here before this gets completely out of control. Are you heading up to your office?"

"Dr. Kilpatrick? One more question."

He squeezed her hand, then nudged her beyond the fringe of the crowd. "I'll hold them back. You go. I'll meet you up there in a few minutes."

"But I heard—"

Another hand closed around her elbow and she flinched. "Come with me, Dr. K. I'll get you out of here."

Boone glared over her head for one quick moment, then dismissed her and her rescuer with a nod before turning away and spreading his arms wide and bellowing to the crowd, "All right, folks, let's see some manners here. Show's over. We're moving toward the front door."

Kate turned and looked into the youthful concern of Pete Estes's blue eyes. Torn by the intellectual need to identify who had spoken that threat to her in the crowd, and the purely instinctive need to get as far away from that threat as possible, she turned toward the chaotic mass one more time—seeking, searching. But she saw nothing but familiar faces she wouldn't suspect and strangers who looked no more threatening than the uniformed officer tugging at her arm.

"This way, ma'am. I've got an elevator waiting."

Sparing one last look at the protective wall of Boone's broad back, standing between her and the danger, she hurried through the elevator doors with Officer Estes. Once inside, he released her. She moved to the side railing to press the third floor button, but he reached past her and pushed the G for the garage level instead.

"Wait, I…" She arched an eyebrow at the young man. What kind of rescuing did he think she needed? "I was going upstairs."

The elevator jerked and began its slow descent.

"Yeah." He unholstered his gun and pointed it at her. "I don't care."

Kate's temperature dropped along with the elevator. But some part of her—the training and intellect—that she relied on when she counseled clients and created criminal profiles kicked in. She slipped her hand into her purse, seeking out the butt of her gun, keeping her nervous energy at bay so that she could think and observe.

It didn't take a profiler or a psychologist to note Pete's wiry build, or how, when she stood in her three-inch heels like this, she could look him straight in the eye.

"Did you get as beat up as I did, Pete, tumbling down the stairs at my house?" The hand holding that gun wasn't that much bigger than her own. "No wonder Pike Taylor's dog went after you. He'd been trailing your scent earlier."

"I thought it was the cat blood. Maybe I hadn't gotten

it all washed off before I answered the neighborhood all-call to secure the scene." He glanced over at Kate, his smile holding no humor. "It was my girlfriend's cat."

"You killed her cat?"

"Thought it'd be less trouble than killing her."

A disturbed young man, indeed. Either he'd lied his way through his psych profile to get into the Academy, or a stress-inducing event was causing him to lose his grasp of right and wrong and reality now. "Pete—"

"Shh." He held a finger to his lips as the elevator stopped. "Not a word. And I'll take that." He slipped her purse—and the gun inside—off her shoulder and tossed it into the corner of the elevator. "When we get off, we're going to walk over to my squad car and we're going to drive out of here."

"There are people working in the garage. Other officers. SWAT Team 1's home base is down here."

He jabbed the gun into her ribs and she winced. "And none of them will get hurt as long as you keep your mouth shut and do what I say."

"Where are we going?" She needed to think—clearly, quickly.

She tucked her hands into her pockets, falling back on the habit of fisting and flexing her fingers there, out of sight, in order to dispel any nervous energy and maintain a calm facade. She fisted a hand in one pocket to keep from crying out loud in relief because, in the other pocket, she discovered another old habit—carrying the important things on her person instead of in her purse. Namely, her cell phone.

She wasn't quite sure what she was going to do with it yet, but she was thinking. As long as she kept her head and didn't panic, she would get out of this. With no more cuts or bruises…or bullet holes. "Pete, I have a meeting to go to upstairs. People are probably already looking for me. This is never going to work."

"I said to stop talking. It just confuses me. It messes everything up. You say all these smart things—they sound good on camera or in some textbook somewhere. But they're not true. They don't work and I'm sick of hearing them." The doors slid open. With his gun hidden beneath his jacket and his free hand wrapped tightly around her arm to keep the gun pressed against her, he pulled her out into the cavernous parking and deployment area for a portion of KCPD's fleet of official vehicles. "Let's walk."

Kate's shoes tapped a familiar staccato on the concrete floor, reminding her of the night she'd heard the man in the brown coveralls following her. There was no longer any stealth to Pete Estes's behavior. His attempts to merely frighten her had escalated into the desire to do her real harm. A sudden shift in the degree of violence he was willing to commit generally meant a psychotic break. She'd been coaching him on his anger issues for a few weeks now, and had seen some progress—in her office. The reality was that something outside her meetings with Pete had triggered the desperate act of kidnapping.

And she had an idea of the cause. "What happened with you and Jeannee? That's your girlfriend's name, isn't it?"

"Ex-girlfriend. No thanks to you." There was the stressor that had triggered his obsessive behavior. He opened the passenger-side door and pushed her into the seat. "Call out to anyone, try to run before I get behind the wheel, and I'll shoot you."

Think, Kate. Think. In the few seconds he took to acknowledge a passing officer and circle around the trunk of the car, Kate pulled out her phone and punched in Boone's number.

She didn't have time for a conversation, couldn't risk an answering ring. Instead, she took a cue from Pete's talent for sending an alarming message in a single word. *Down.*

Kate texted the word, hit Send as the car door opened, dropped the phone back into her pocket and prayed Boone was as smart as he was caring and protective and funny and… The car door closed.

"Where are we going?" she asked again. Although she had a pretty good idea.

"To talk some sense into Jeannee." After shifting the car into Drive, he pulled the gun out and set it on his thigh, reminding Kate the he was armed and she was not. Reminding her, too, that she was the only one in the squad car who was thinking rationally right now. "And if you don't make things right between us, then I'm going to shoot you both."

WITH THE LOBBY AREA CLEARING OUT and the KCPD crew taking control of that crazy mob that had swarmed around Kate, Boone stepped out of the way to let the city cops escort the reporters and drama seekers outside. He wondered what his chances were of convincing Kate to let someone else, who wasn't the target of some crazy guy's threats, take over the public spotlight.

And sure, she'd kept her cool on the outside when the questions had taken a personal turn. But he'd seen the hands disappear. He knew her skin wasn't as thick as she'd like the rest of the world to think it was. He knew what it cost her to face down Vanessa Owen and the memories of an unpleasant past.

Let somebody else take the hits. Let somebody else deal with the grabbing hands and taking the blame for unsolved crimes that had the city on edge.

He wanted Kate Kilpatrick away from all this mess. He wanted her safe.

Boone pressed the elevator button, thinking he'd have at least three floors to come up with some reasonable argument to get Kate to hide away someplace safe for a while—preferably in bed with him. She'd probably acknowledge his argument, come back with some logical counterargument, distract him with the brush of her hand over his arm, and then stubbornly go about doing whatever she thought was right—no matter what it cost her.

Or him.

The elevator opened and Boone stepped inside. He pushed the button for the third floor, glanced down and saw the leather purse crumpled in the corner.

Boone's blood ran cold. He scooped up the familiar bag, caught the sliding door and shoved it back open.

A quick sweep of the lobby and dwindling crowd told him she wasn't here.

"Doc?"

He'd taken a couple of steps toward the front doors to follow the press conference attendees outside when his phone beeped.

He paused to read the incoming text from Kate's phone. "Down." What did that mean?

Boone mentally replayed the last few seconds he'd had Kate in his sights. Final statement. Crowd. Swarm.

Hand on her. Push her toward elevator. She braced her hand against him and…

"She saw something." No. Some*one*.

Boone grabbed the first blue suit that walked by. "What's downstairs?"

He flashed his badge before the officer would answer. "The SWAT garage, equipment storage, squad car parking—"

"Any way to get there besides the elevator?"

The officer pointed to the stairs.

Boone shoved open the door and hit the stairwell. He dialed Spencer Montgomery's number and unholstered his Glock as he waited for the detective to pick up.

"This is Montgomery."

"Code red or blue or whatever you call it here. Get a team down to the basement." Boone shoved open the door at the foot of the stairs. "That Estes kid just took Kate."

Chapter Ten

The cage was coming down over the garage's exit arch.

"What the…?" Pete stomped on the brake of the speeding car. Kate braced her hands and they skidded to the edge of the ramp leading up to the street. "What did you do, Dr. K.?"

They lurched to a stop and Pete's gun toppled to the floorboards. For two milliseconds, Kate considered diving for the weapon herself. But by the time she'd released her death grip on the dashboard and reached for the door handle, Pete had already retrieved the gun and aimed it squarely at Kate's chest.

"Don't you move!"

Kate also saw the silhouette of a cowboy hat in the side view mirror. She turned in her seat as he came up beside the car, with his gun cradled between both hands. "Oh, no, no, no. Boone, wait!"

There were other guns. Too many guns. Detectives Montgomery and Fensom. Maggie Wheeler. She'd texted for help and the cavalry had arrived.

Boone darted up to the front fender and pointed his gun at the driver behind the windshield. "Get out of the car, Estes!"

More movement in the mirror and to her left warned

Kate they were being surrounded. Men she recognized from SWAT Team 1 were slipping into flak vests and aiming rifles.

This wasn't going to end well.

Unless someone with a cool head prevailed.

Kate held her arms up in surrender. Her hands were shaking. She kept her head slightly bowed although she never completely looked away from Pete or the gun.

"Estes!" Boone shouted.

"I need to roll my window down so I can talk to him, Pete, okay? I'll tell him to lower his weapon." She brought her hands back to her lap, softened her voice. "I'm not going anywhere."

Pete's hands were shaking, too.

"Please, Pete." If she was right, this desperate young man didn't really want to harm her. He'd been frustrated, maybe even scared, angry for sure. He'd needed someone to blame for his troubles, someone to pay for his girlfriend leaving, and Kate—the woman who was supposed to fix all that for him and had failed—had become the target of all those unbalanced emotions.

She inhaled a deep, silent breath, trying to stay focused, trying to calm her nerves, trying to remember everything she'd ever learned about talking to someone as troubled as Pete Estes.

He glanced through the glass at Boone's rock-steady hands, then back at her. "Tell him to drop his gun."

Moving slowly so as not to alarm Pete, Kate rolled down the passenger window. The fumes from the garage stung her nose as she leaned her head toward the opening. "Boone, please put your gun away."

"When he tosses his out of the car."

"Please," she begged. She watched the emotions

travel across his face. He was a man of action. He'd promised to protect her. Holstering his gun and letting her take control of the potentially deadly standoff must be like her letting go of her emotions and simply trusting her instincts. She looked up at the tic of a muscle working beneath his steeled jaw. "Pete just needs to talk."

"He should have made an appointment." His eyes never left Pete or the gun trained on her. "Are you hurt?"

"No." She had to make Boone understand that this was one problem that violence couldn't solve. She had to make Pete understand that, too. "I need everyone to put their guns away."

"You have to fix it with Jeannee." Pete's gun continued to shake. "I said all those things you told me to. I told her I was going to be okay about the baby, that we'd make it work. But you lied, Dr. Kilpatrick. She left me anyway." He ground the gun against her shoulder. "She left me."

"Kate?"

"No!" She warned Boone back.

"He left all those damn threats, didn't he? He hurt you that night at the house."

"I'm fine. I need you to trust me on this." She tore her gaze away from Boone and read the desperation in Pete's eyes. "Pete just wants someone to listen. He wanted me to stop talking and listen."

Pete's head jerked with a nod.

"I'm listening now."

It was the first hint of trust, the first sign of being able to reason with him—her first hope that she and Pete both might get out of this squad car alive. Kate leaned her head out the window again. "I need Jean-nee Mercer, Tiger Village Apartments, on the phone right now."

Nick Fensom, standing off to the side in her peripheral vision, holstered his weapon and pulled out his phone. "I'm on it."

"She may not want to talk." Kate didn't know if Pete had physically abused his girlfriend. But she was guessing that with his anger management issues, she'd certainly borne the brunt of his verbal tirades.

Nick nodded his understanding and retreated. "I'll make it happen."

"I need everyone to put their guns away," she said.

The Glock in Boone's outstretched hands must be getting heavy, but he hadn't wavered.

Despite the facts, Kate tried to assure him she had the situation under control. "This isn't a kidnapping, it's a…counseling session."

"Don't make me put my gun away."

"Please, Boone." She saw the sweat beading on his upper lip. "I'll ask Pete to lower his weapon, too."

She looked to the younger man, dropped her gaze to the gun bruising her shoulder. "How about it?"

He pulled the gun from the dent he'd made in her sleeve and the skin beneath. The gun still rested on his thigh, but it was pointed in a less vulnerable position toward her legs. "Thank you." She forced her trembling lips to smile. "See? It's okay."

"All right." At last, he eased his stance and slowly, keeping his hands where Pete could see them, slipped his gun into its holster. He inched closer to her window. "But you're not gettin' rid of me."

It was a promise she wanted to cling to, a promise she was starting to believe.

"Let me ask you a question, Boone." It was a natural excuse for him to move another step closer to her window. "Pete. You and Sheriff Harrison have a lot in common."

"Like what?" he sneered. "If you're gonna talk, you'd better make those words count."

She intended to. "You're both officers of the law. And pretty good ones, too, I think."

She glanced up at Boone, urging him to say something helpful. His handsome mouth was a tight line of doubt. "Yeah, Estes. I've been in this business for almost twenty years. I'm sure you've got a long career ahead of you, too."

Kate slid her hand along the door above the armrest. She wanted to touch Boone, to squeeze his hand, to borrow his strength. But a firmer grip on Pete's gun warned her to pull her hand back to her lap. "Being married to a cop isn't easy. Being in a relationship with one doesn't always work out."

"Kate…" Boone cautioned. It was a risky topic, for both men. Yet she knew there was no one here who could understand Pete Estes's situation better than Boone.

"Sheriff Harrison's wife left him. Like Jeannee left you."

Boone was catching on to her ploy long before Pete. "Yeah, um…the long hours are hard for someone who isn't in the business."

"Sometimes, you're working so hard to establish your career, that you may lose track of what's going on at home."

Pete agreed. "Jeannee said I wasn't spending enough time with her. I didn't help her paint the baby's room."

The other detectives and uniformed officers surrounding the car were slowly lowering their weapons and backing off. But Kate could see it was because the SWAT team was fully armed now and getting into more strategic positions. Kate had to keep Pete talking to distract him from their movements. "I'm sure you feel as badly about that as she does."

"I felt guilty as hell. I want to take care of my boy… or little girl. But I need to spend time on the streets, too." He ducked his head to see Boone through her window. "I have to earn the respect of the people on my beat."

Boone nodded, pretending he and Pete were sharing a moment of camaraderie. "You have to get to know them."

"Right. It takes time. My shift may say I get off in eight hours, but if there's something I have to take care of…"

"You can't leave victims in the middle of a traffic accident." Boone was a natural at getting the rookie officer to talk. "If a crime is in progress, you have to stop it. You can't wait for the next guy to do it for you."

"Exactly. I want to be with Jeannee. But I want to do my job right, too. How else can I get promoted and make more money? I'm going to have a family to support."

Nick Fensom returned to the car, with his hands and cell phone up in the air. Pete raised his gun again and Kate held her breath. "I've got her." Nick had Jeannee Mercer—and the possible end to this standoff—on the line. "I reached her at her mother's place."

Her breath eased out on a careful sigh. "May I take the phone from Detective Fensom?"

"Yeah." Pete was waving the gun again, but this time, it was Boone who held up his hands to warn the SWAT team to hold their fire. "But Cowboy there steps back."

"I explained the situation," Nick said, handing Kate the phone. "She said she'd come down to the precinct. I sent Sgt. Wheeler out to pick her up."

Kate put the cell to her ear and introduced herself. "I'm Dr. Kilpatrick. I'm a…friend of Pete's. He'd like to say how much he loves you. And explain a few things to you."

"Jeannee?" Pete took the phone after an encouraging nod from Kate. "Yeah, baby. I love you, too. I don't want you to be afraid of me. I want to do better by you." The young man was laughing, crying, setting his gun down on his thigh and finally relaxing his guard the more he talked. "I need you to understand where I'm coming from."

They talked for seven minutes and twenty-three seconds, according to the dashboard clock.

At seven minutes and twenty-four seconds, Pete let go of his gun to switch the cell to his right hand.

Enough talking. Kate snatched the gun from his lap. Boone opened her door and pulled her from the car, forcing her down against the protection of the tire and fender and shielding her body with his while the SWAT team swooped in to drag Pete from the car. They put him facedown on the concrete and cuffed his wrists behind his back.

When the SWAT team commander, Michael Cutler, announced the all-clear, Boone pressed his lips against

Kate's ear and whispered, "You probably just saved that kid's life. But next time, Doc? We do things my way."

Kate was shaking so badly when they stood up that Boone was the only thing holding her upright. She curled her fingers into the sleeve of his jacket and held on.

And that was when she realized that Boone was shaking, too.

"THE HEROINE OF THE DAY."

When would the madness end?

Boone closed the conference room door as a round of applause from Spencer Montgomery and the members of the task force greeted Kate's arrival at the late-afternoon meeting. He was bone tired and itching to get someplace where he wasn't running into another cop or reporter who wanted to get close to Kate to either congratulate her for talking her way out of a hostage crisis or get a quote for the evening news and morning paper.

Kate should be in a bed, sleeping.

No, she should be in a safehouse bed, catching up on her sleep.

And if he was in that bed with her, so much the better.

He could tell by the extra-determined tilt of her chin that she was exhausted by the emotional ordeal of the last few days, too. She was working that sophisticated ice-princess facade while he was feeling more raw and less refined than ever after watching that sad, mixed-up kid hold a gun on her. He'd had the shot. He could have taken the young officer out. But Kate had insisted on saving her client's neck as well as her own.

She smiled at their praise and thanked them for their

concern before sitting down at the long table. Boone dropped his hat on top of the table and pulled out a chair to sit beside her, not waiting for an invitation to join the meeting. He'd agreed to be Kate's protector in exchange for access to the task force's investigation.

Until Janie's killer was locked behind bars, and these people could prove that the only danger stalking Kate was now locked away in a psych evaluation cell, he was staying.

"You should hear the press buzzing now," said Spencer Montgomery. Kate audibly groaned at the prospect of going another round with local reporters. "Don't worry. Chief Taylor is taking care of them. I'm relieving you of press liaison duty, Kate."

"'Bout damn time," Boone muttered under his breath.

The detective at the head of the table paused at the interruption. "I hate to say it, but Sheriff Harrison was right. Setting you up as the bait to draw out Estes turned out to be far more dangerous than any risk I'm comfortable with."

"Pete Estes is a troubled young man." Kate still wanted to defend this guy? "If he'd gotten out of the garage with me as a hostage, I'm guessing one or both of us would have died in an inevitable shoot-out. He's confused and hurting and needs a lot of help." She looked to every person sitting around the table, including Boone. Perhaps her gaze lingered a little longer on him. "Thank you for letting me take charge of the situation."

"You've done good work, Kate," Montgomery said. "Your theory about multiple unsubs was right. Estes had a personal beef with you, and tried to cover his tracks with the red roses. But he isn't our rapist or killer."

"I don't think he even knows Janie Harrison's name. His focus was on his girlfriend, and then on me because he blamed me for her leaving him."

"You're eliminating all kinds of suspects for us, Kate. The victim's boyfriend. This copycat stalker." With a nod to the criminologist sitting across from Boone, Montgomery continued. "But I'd pay good money if someone could bring me a viable suspect on this case. We're no closer to identifying the Rose Red Rapist than we were a week ago. Annie?"

Annie Hermann stood to set her big shoulder bag on top of the table with a solid thunk. She pulled out one file after another, sorting through the labels until she found the one she was looking for and handed it off to Maggie Wheeler. "Here. I have the results we've been waiting for from the lab. I know chemical analysis reports can be hard to read, but go ahead and pass them around. I made a copy for everybody."

"And what do these squiggly lines mean to those of us who aren't scientists?" Nick asked, passing the folder around the table.

Boone was willing to back up the five foot two inches of glare Annie shot toward Nick, providing it would either (a) get Kate out of this meeting and into the comparative safety and privacy of their hotel room sooner, or (b) give him the answers he needed to finally let his sister rest in peace.

"I've been working on identifying the silver trace the M.E. found in Jane Harrison's hair."

The folder finally made its way around to him. He remembered a few abbreviations from chemistry class, but he wasn't seeing the familiar symbol for silver on the report. "The heirloom necklace Janie wore was sterling silver."

"Right." Annie pointed to the photo of the tiny, round-cornered square of metal. "That's not sterling. Or even low-grade silver. It's stainless steel. So…" She reached into her bag and pulled out a molded piece of plaster sculpture. "This is the cast I made of the victim's head wound. I'm not sure exactly what it is yet, but this is the weapon that killed your sister. And I believe whatever it is was made out of stainless steel."

Boone picked up the three-dimensional re-creation of the blunt object that had taken Janie's life. It was two-pronged and cylindrical in shape, about the size of his fist. He remembered the M.E. saying it looked like the object had impaled Janie's head when she'd been struck. The two curved prongs protruding at the end were certainly long enough to do that.

"May I see that?" Kate held out her hand and Boone placed the odd-shaped object into her palm. She picked up the photo of the stainless shard and placed it at the end of the shorter prong.

"It fits, doesn't it," Annie reported. "It's a piece that broke off the tip of the weapon."

"Ideas on what it could be?" Montgomery asked.

Kate's shoulders sagged beside him while the others tossed out suggestions of tools and knickknacks. Her skin turned ashen, save for the bruise on her cheek. Boone ignored the decorum of the meeting and slipped his hand behind her back. "Are you all right?"

She turned her eyes up to his, but the soft green irises were focused someplace far away.

"Kate?" Boone's weary muscles rejuvenated with

concern. Meeting or not, he was taking her out of here to get some rest.

But then she sat up straight and turned to Spencer Montgomery. "Did you get that list of motel guests from the night Janie called there?"

"Yes." He thumbed through his leather binder and pulled out the paper. "Here."

She snatched it from Montgomery's hand and skimmed through the list. Everyone was watching her now. Her shoulders dipped again, but then her chin tilted up.

Boone gripped the arm of his chair, waiting for the grim pronouncement stamped across her features. "My theory about a second unsub is still correct. I don't know who our rapist is yet, but I know who killed Jane Harrison." She set down the list in front of him and pointed to a name. "So do you."

Chapter Eleven

"It matches."

Kate had never wanted to be more wrong about a thing in her life. She'd wanted to be wrong about her husband and good friend's affair. She'd wanted to be wrong about Pete Estes and had almost hoped she had the real Rose Red Rapist stalking her instead of a young man so confused and angry about his world that he believed his only outlet was to terrorize her. For Boone's sake, she'd wanted to be wrong about his sister being involved with a married man, repeating the same pattern that had once destroyed his life.

She really wanted to be wrong about this.

But her mind was too sharp. She remembered too many impressions about people. She could never quite shut off that always-thinking-always-evaluating brain of hers.

Kate wrapped the collar of her brown trench coat higher around her neck and hunched down against the stiff wind whipping along Nichols Street, just off the courthouse square in Grangeport, Missouri. She held up the photograph of Annie Hermann's two-pronged murder weapon beside the taillight of Flint Larson's green pickup truck, parked in front of the Alton County Sheriff's Department.

The object in Annie's photo was three-dimensional, but the design was the same.

A rearing stallion. Handmade with love by an artist who enjoyed sculpting in metal. Long mane flying in the wind. Two shapely, slender front legs, curling out from its muscular body. The fragment of stainless steel that had caught in Janie Harrison's hair was the tip of a hoof that had broken off when her head struck Flint's truck.

"I'm sorry, Boone." Kate looked over at the broad-shouldered sheriff, pushing his Stetson more firmly onto his head to withstand the bleak promise of winter blowing through town. Her heart went out to him standing there in stoic silence, his brooding stare fixed on the back of his deputy and good friend's truck.

How did a man stand that kind of betrayal from a friend? From someone he trusted?

Kate knew. And she didn't wish that kind of pain on anyone.

Spencer Montgomery was on his phone, ignorant or uncaring of what the evidence meant to the local sheriff. "I'll get a search warrant for Larson's truck, his home and his office. Looks like there's a decorative ornament missing from the hitch. Let's start snapping some pictures. Sheriff, do you have an address on this guy?"

At last Boone spoke. "You're in my jurisdiction now, Montgomery." His world-weary gaze swept over Kate, too, giving a double meaning to his words. "We do this *my* way."

"Maybe there's another explanation. Someone borrowed Flint's truck or…" Kate took a step toward him, but Boone's hard look kept her from taking another.

"We're not dragging this out. We're not talking it through all day long. The evidence is there. I need to take care of this for Janie."

Spencer put his call on hold and turned around to face him. "You're not talking about some kind of vigilante justice, are you?" He didn't back off the way Kate had. "To flip a phrase you once threw in my face—I don't know how you do things here in Grangeport, but in Kansas City we build a case against a suspect. Then we arrest him and make it stick."

"We do the same thing here in Grangeport, Detective." Boone was moving now, checking the gun and badge and handcuffs on his belt, striding toward the office's front door. "Flint's probably out on a call in a departmental vehicle right now. You make your case. I'll bring him in."

"Boone." Kate caught his arm as he walked past. "You're asking an awful lot of yourself. A good friend murdered your sister."

"And I want to know why. I want him to tell me to my face how he could do this to my Janie."

She shook her head. "You're too close to this. Too angry. Let Spencer do it."

"No."

"Then at least let me come with you."

"Doc…"

He looked her up and down, from the sweep of her bangs down to her jeans and high-heeled boots. And when she thought he was about to make some excuse about how she wasn't dressed for traipsing around the countryside after a murder suspect, he slid his hand beneath the fringe of hair at her nape, angled her head back and kissed her. It was hard and deep and thorough and fast, and Kate latched on to his collar and stretched up to answer with the same raw need inside her.

And then her heels were flat on the ground and Boone's thumb gave a rough stroke over her bottom lip. "I nearly lost you yesterday to one man who was willing to kill the people I love. I'm not going to give anybody else the chance to do it again.

"You stay."

The people I love?

Boone's parting words fueled Kate's steps as she paced circles around the wood-paneled lobby of the Alton County Sheriff's Station. Boone loved her? Or had that been a generic statement about home territory and losing his sister and not being emotionally prepared to deal with another loss?

He loved her?

A good man. An honest man. A loyal, caring man. A man who could kiss her like she was the most precious, fragile thing on earth one minute, and then in the next minute make her feel like the sexiest, most desirable woman he'd ever met. He made her feel safe. He made her feel unsure. He made her feel…period.

A man like that loved her?

"Why would I say something if I didn't mean it?"

"Not everyone who makes a promise keeps it."

"I do."

Kate stopped in her tracks. She stopped thinking. For once, she stood still and simply *felt* the truth. Boone Harrison loved her.

And she… *Let the past go. Embrace the woman you*

are now, the woman Boone sees. "Don't think it, Kate," she whispered. "Feel it."

She inhaled a deep, cleansing breath, ready to take a leap of faith. "I—"

"Kate!" Spencer Montgomery ran out of Boone's office with another deputy charging behind him. "We have to go."

"Go where?" She grabbed her coat off the bench beside the front door and shrugged her arms into it. "I thought we were meeting Boone here. That he was bringing Flint to us."

The deputy was already out the door, revving the throttle of his departmental SUV and peeling off down the street.

"There's been a change in plans." Spencer opened the door and hurried her outside to his car. "I promised him I wouldn't leave you alone here. Do you have your weapon?"

"In my purse."

"I'd keep it closer than that."

A fist of dread punched her in the stomach. "You talked to Boone? What's wrong?"

"He just called." Kate buckled her seat belt as Spencer mounted a magnetic siren on the roof of his car and took off after the deputy's speeding SUV.

"There's been a situation with Larson."

"What?"

"Do you know what a Mexican standoff is?"

"Yes, when two people hold guns…" Kate's stomach dropped to her feet. "Oh, my God."

"Yeah. Larson's refusing to come in."

"THAT'S CLOSE ENOUGH, Doc."

The Missouri River bluffs in the autumn really were beautiful, Boone thought obliquely, as he adjusted his stance behind a pile of dead pines that had been cut and stacked for burning. But the bluffs paled in comparison to Dr. Kate Kilpatrick picking her way through a stubble of cow pasture to reach the trees near the hunting blind where Flint Larson had holed up. She had burrs stuck to her jeans, dust on her once shiny boots and a Glock on her belt. A KCPD flak vest from Spencer Montgomery's trunk weighed down the naturally erect posture of her body.

"Not another step, Doc." She might be armed, but she herself had said she didn't carry a weapon regularly, and he wasn't sure how well she'd be able to defend herself if her request to talk Flint Larson out of his suicidal threats went south. "Stick to the cover of the trees."

She glanced over her shoulder. "I don't want to be shouting at him."

And he didn't want her close enough where Flint could put his hands on her, either—or where she could take a tumble over the granite and limestone cliffs into the churning muddy water below their position.

"Come on out, Flint," Boone shouted, urging him once again to step out into the open and surrender himself. "KCPD's here now. Please, buddy. Don't make us come in there with our guns. I worry one of us won't make it back out that way."

Flint shouted from inside the stacked lumber and canvas of the blind. "One of us *won't* make it out, Boone. You know that."

"Flint? It's Kate Kilpatrick. Remember that chat we had the day of Janie's funeral?"

"Get out of here, lady!" Flint warned. "I'm not in the mood to talk."

"I remember our conversation. You were quite charming." Kate was some twenty yards ahead and to the west, about halfway between his Glock and Flint's Smith & Wesson, but out of the direct crossfire should this request and refusal to come in and face the charges against him get any more screwed up than they already had.

"That's bull, and you know it." A nearly empty whiskey bottle came hurtling out of the blind toward Kate's position and Boone jerked inside his boots, fighting the instinct to go get her and bring her back out of harm's way. "I'm not coming out, boss."

Perhaps sensing his impulse, Kate looked back to him and held up a placating hand, asking him to stay back. Stubborn woman. She wouldn't be deterred from trying to talk Boone's deputy out of his hidey-hole. She leaned up against the trunk of a crooked pin oak and tried again. "What if I talk for a minute, Flint, and you just listen?"

When Flint didn't answer, she darted up to hide behind the next tree. "Kate," Boone warned.

He knew she was good at this sort of thing—and that he wasn't. But she was just too damn close.

But knowing she was treading on dangerous ground with the Rose Red Rapist case and that crazy kid of a stalker hadn't stopped her yet, the unpredictable danger of a drunken, suicidal man who was armed with at least one gun wouldn't stop her, either. "We know Janie's death was an accident, Flint."

"It wasn't!" he argued, his voice growing more and

more slurred by the alcohol he'd consumed. "I'm sorry, boss. I killed her. I got so damn mad. I pushed and..."

And what? Could he stand here, hiding in the trees, and listen to how his innocent baby sister had fallen victim to someone she trusted? Boone's breath stilled in his chest. But he found Kate's eyes looking back at him, comforting him, calming him, and he found he could breathe again.

"Tell us what happened, Flint." As much as he hated putting her in harm's way on purpose, Boone was praying that she could work another miracle and talk his longtime friend into surrendering his gun. But she was getting nothing but silence.

"Kate, come on back." He couldn't take this. He was beat up inside with love and worry for that woman. He needed her back here where he could put his hands on her and keep her safe. "When night comes, the cold will chase him out."

"Flint?"

Boone swore when he saw Kate inch up to another tree. Screw hanging back. Keeping low to the ground, Boone crept out from behind his cover and ducked into the same copse of oaks where she was positioned. If she wouldn't come to him, then he was going after her. Again. "Doc, you're scaring me. This was a bad idea. At least draw your weapon so you can defend yourself."

Thank God she at least followed that directive. She slowly unsnapped her holster and pulled the Glock into her hands while she kept talking in that calm, even tone of hers.

"We've already matched your truck to the head wound that killed Janie." But she wasn't any more willing to give up on the idea of getting Flint out of here alive than he was. "There are KCPD criminologists and detectives at your house right now, Flint, searching for evidence that you were there that night with Janie."

"They won't find anything." Finally, an answer.

Even Boone froze where he stood.

"Why not?" Kate asked.

"Because I have it here with me." And with that, Flint stumbled out of the blind with his Smith & Wesson in his hand. Boone's gun went up instantly. He closed one eye, getting a bead on the deputy. But Boone's aim wavered slightly when Flint held up the other hand, dangling the silver heirloom necklace from his fingers.

Ah, hell. Flint had killed Janie. There was no longer even a smidgen of hope left inside him that Kate and the task force and their evidence might be wrong. Boone could hear Montgomery and the deputies moving through the dry grass behind him. And every last man was armed, every bullet was aimed at Flint.

"Drop your weapon, Flint," Boone ordered. "As your friend. As your superior officer—"

"I've washed my truck a dozen times since that night." Boone peeked around the tree as Flint's slurred voice came closer. "But I can't get rid of the blood. It's in my head and on my hands and in my heart. I can't clean it all out of me."

"Kate, pull back," Boone warned.

She started to move, but Flint swung his gun around toward her.

"Kate!"

She jumped back and hugged her body close to the tree again.

"You were right, Doctor." She had Flint talking now. "I was Kate's confidant. I'm the good friend she called that night. I drove all the way to Kansas City to fix the problem for her."

"Fix the problem?" Boone swore. "She'd been raped. Why didn't you take her to the police? Or a hospital? Why didn't you call me?"

"She didn't want her brothers to know just how badly she'd screwed up. But she trusted me. She needed me!"

"Being raped is an act of violence, not a mistake a woman makes. I know you loved her," Kate said gently, urging Flint to quiet his temper. "You told me you went to help her whenever she asked. You were a good friend to her. Even after she broke off your engagement. Not many men have the character to do that."

Boone tried to move closer to Kate, to get her back to safety. But Flint swung the gun back toward him and fired three shots down into the ground, pinning him.

"Flint, stop!" Kate shouted. "You'll only make it worse. Put down your gun. I'll talk with you for as long as you want. Just put down your gun."

Flint took a lurching step toward Kate's position. "I loved her. And I thought…"

Boone flattened his back against the tree. Montgomery and the others were too far back. He had to get to Kate before Flint did.

"Keep him talking, Doc."

"You shut up!" Another pair of shots hit the bark beside Boone, throwing a chip of wood across his cheek and drawing blood.

"Flint!"

Boone peered around the tree. "I'm okay, Doc. Get back."

But the woman thought she could talk her way out

of anything. She thought she could help a drunken lost soul like Flint. She thought she needed to protect him.

She had her hands and gun up in the air and was walking into the clearing toward Flint. "Just talk to me, Flint. Okay? Look at me." *No, honey. No, no, no!* She stooped and set her gun on the ground, turning herself into an easy target. "See? I'm not armed. I just want to talk. That's it."

Boone caught Spencer Montgomery's eye and silently gave him the order to circle around behind Flint's blind side. Kate was still in the open. But if she hit the ground when he told her to, Montgomery would have a clear shot to take out Boone's friend.

He hadn't wanted it to come to this. Flint had been halfway to drunk by the time Boone had found him and explained the evidence KCPD had against him. The man had broken down into tears of guilt and regret and penance—or so Boone had believed. He'd let him go to the john to wash his face. The next thing he'd heard instead of running water was the sound of an ATV motor, tearing off across the countryside. Boone had driven his truck as far as the landscape would let him, and then followed on foot. The chase had ended here.

He'd been worried Flint wouldn't surrender.

Now he was beginning to worry about something even worse.

"Kate! You come back to me." Boone smeared the blood off his cheek. He pulled off his hat and tossed it into the grass at his feet, giving himself a slimmer profile, making himself a harder target to hit. He flexed his fingers around the grip of his Glock, mentally preparing himself for where this showdown might be headed.

"If anything happens to her, Flint, you are not leaving here alive."

"It's okay, Boone." How could Kate sound so sweet and calm when his heart was tied up like a branding calf inside his chest? "Flint and I are just talking. Right? Tell me more about that night."

"I went to Kansas City to see her. Janie said she was in trouble and so I went." Flint's throat grew froggy from tears and drink. "I got us a motel room so we could have some privacy. She was all messed up, like she'd been in a fight." Tears burned beneath Boone's own eyelids at all the sad mistakes that had led to such a tragedy that night. "I thought that boyfriend—Max or whatever she called him—had hurt her. I got so mad. I wanted to go after him. But she came out of the room after me. To stop me. She said she loved him. That it would break her heart if I hurt him. She told me she wanted to call him for help, but she couldn't because he had a wife. She was defending him to me!" Boone didn't have to see Flint to understand the rage building inside him. "She called *me* for help. I thought he'd done that to her. Yet she kept going on and on—Max, Max, Max."

"You fought?"

Boone heard a sorrowful gasp, like the last breath of a dying animal. It was Flint. "I didn't mean to. But I pushed—she fell. She hit her head on the hitch of my truck. The one she'd made for me. There was so much blood. She was gone."

"And afterward?"

"I kept the necklace because it always meant so much to her."

Boone risked another peek around the tree. He

swiped the tears from his vision. Kate was right there, close enough for Flint to touch her. *Move, woman,* he begged, silently creeping toward them. *Give me a clear shot.*

"I took her body back to that alley where I'd picked her up. Left the rose with her like that guy had." One step. Another step. "I loved her." Flint shook his head. "I killed her."

"Put the gun down, Flint," Kate asked quietly. "There are cops all around you. Please put the gun down."

"Kate, get down!" Boone shouted, moving out of the trees, raising his gun.

And then the nightmare happened.

Drunk and unsteady, but strong and desperate enough to react to the threat, Flint grabbed Kate, hugged her and the bulletproof vest in front of him and put the gun to her head.

Kate screamed. Boone charged forward until he didn't dare take another step.

If Flint had pointed the gun at him, he wouldn't have hesitated to shoot. But he had Kate.

"Don't make me do this, Flint. It's suicide."

His deputy smiled. "Don't you think I know that, boss?"

"Damn it, Flint. You could have surrendered."

"And live with knowin' what I did to Janie? And to you?"

Kate thought there was still a chance to reach him. "Flint, please."

"No, ma'am. No more." Flint turned the gun to his own head.

"Flint, no," Kate gasped.

"You're right. He won't shoot to save me." He moved the gun back to her temple. "But he'll save you."

"Don't make me," Boone begged. "Let her go."

"Can't do that, boss."

Montgomery shouted from his position. "Cowboy, you got a plan?"

"Yes." Boone's gun never wavered. He looked straight into Kate's beautiful eyes. "I love you."

"I love you," she answered without hesitation, and something warm and perfect and too good to lose blossomed inside him.

"I'll do it, boss." Flint ground the gun into her temple, forcing her head to the side.

"Yeah, Doc. But do you trust me?"

Boone waited. He aimed. He held his breath.

"Yes."

Boone pulled the trigger. He hit Flint in the middle of his forehead and the man who'd killed his sister, who'd threatened the woman he loved, who'd lied, crumpled to the ground. Dead.

BOONE LACED HIS FINGERS TOGETHER with Kate's and walked her to the barn to introduce her to Big Jim and the other horses. She might not know how to ride yet, but she sure had an affinity for petting foreheads and combing manes and holding carrots out in the flat of her hand for long tongues and soft muzzles to gobble up.

A week had passed since Flint Larson's funeral. A lifetime had passed, it seemed, since he'd nearly lost her to a pair of dangerous young men. One, she'd used her skills of talking and listening and thinking on her feet to escape from. The other, he'd used his more instinctive abilities to escape the promise of death. Thank

God she'd finally decided to take him at his word and trusted him to take that shot.

They'd shared their darkest secrets, some incredible passion, and their hearts. She wasn't afraid to get her shoes muddy or tell him to get his filthy boots out of the kitchen.

But Boone's world wasn't perfect. Not yet.

He pulled her to the ladder leading up to the loft and kissed her hand. "Have you ever had a roll in the hay, Dr. Kate?"

"Can't say as I have."

"It beats a hot bubble bath or a long ride on a horse."

She put her foot on the first rung of the ladder, looked over her shoulder and smiled. "Well, it's been a very long, very stressful week. And I think we both need to…decompress."

Boone palmed her butt to hurry her on up the ladder and climbed up behind her. "I like the way you think, Doc."

She liked the quilt he'd spread out over the hay, and the wine and cheese-and-crackers, and condom he'd already set into place, too. "Hmm…this country living has more going for it than I'd ever suspected."

Boone uncorked the wine and picked up the two glasses to pour a little something to set the mood. "We can class it up like you city sophisticates if we have to."

And then he nearly dropped the glasses when he felt her arms sliding around him from behind. "I'm not thirsty, Boone." She flicked his hat off into the hay and brushed her lips against the back of his neck. "I'm not hungry, either."

He set down the wine and goblet, then turned to

gather her in his arms. "I'm starving," he confessed before claiming her mouth with his.

The talking stopped as greedy hands and hungry kisses took over. Boots dropped. Coats and belts and clothes disappeared. Kate's hands skimmed his body, sending shivers through him. She coaxed his nipples to attention, teased their painful tightness with the swirl of her tongue. She drew her nails along his spine and squeezed his butt as he laved her beautiful breasts and sucked the pink tips into pebbled flowers. She wound a firm hand around his swollen manhood and urged him toward her welcoming heat.

He laid her back across the quilt. The crinkle of hay strands breaking beneath them, along with her sweet, moaning gasps, made music in the air. The exotic scent of jasmine in her hair erased the pungent smells of the barn, filling his head with Kate and her giving hands and heart.

When he couldn't stand another moment of being incomplete, Boone entered Kate in a swift, deep thrust. She wound her legs around his hips, hugged her arms around his shoulders, threaded her fingers into his hair. Those sweet green eyes looked up into his for a moment before she tipped her head back and cried out his name. Boone buried his face against her throat and held on as his body tensed at the brink of satisfaction. And then her hands clutched at his back and he toppled over with the roar of his release. He couldn't imagine anything more perfect than being with Kate Kilpatrick.

Now she was in his arms, snuggling close as the autumn air cooled their bare skin. And those sexy hands were trailing leisurely lines up and down his chest and abdomen.

Boone caught her hand and stilled it over his heart before she made him forget why they'd needed to decompress in the first place. "You're not gettin' rid of me, Doc. You know that, right?"

"I'm not trying to." She pushed herself up on one elbow, her kiss-stung mouth marred by a serious frown. "But your job is here. Mine's in Kansas City. I'm not quitting that task force until the Rose Red Rapist is off the streets and the women in Kansas City are safe again."

"I don't want you to quit."

"You live on a ranch and I live in a house that's too big for me—"

"And we both have some emotional healing left to do. I know." He lifted his head and kissed her until that frown eased into a hopeful smile. "We've talked about this before, Doc. We've both been married to people who were with us every day, and yet they didn't stay."

"So how are we going to make us work?" She gently touched the cut healing on his cheek. "Because I really want us to work."

"I want us to work, too." He brushed a fingertip across the fading bruise on *her* cheek. "Whether I go to K.C. and whip those city cops into shape or you come here to Grangeport and give it some uptown class, I want to be with you."

"Well…" He saw the wheels turning inside her head, knew that woman was thinking of something that could change his world. Again.

Boone let his head fall back to the quilt with a resigned sigh. "What?"

"Maybe if you just promise me that we'll keep working on this relationship, I'll believe it. It doesn't have to be perfect right now. But we'll figure it out so that one day soon it will be."

Boone smiled and pulled her down on top of him. "Whatever we do, Doc—we do it together. I promise."

Epilogue

The man turned off the television and laughed.

"What's so funny?"

Everything in him tensed as the woman walked up behind his chair. He hated when she did that. She knew him so well in so many ways that he couldn't do without her. Yet every now and then he got the idea that he didn't know her as well as he should.

He gestured to the chair across from him, inviting her to sit. Picking up some papers from his desk, he sorted through them, making sure they were in order.

"Well?" she prompted.

He didn't like that, either, when she made even small demands like that from him. His nostrils flared as he forced himself to maintain an even rhythm of breathing. Maintaining his anonymity often required a great deal of patience and pretending he didn't care about things as deeply as he did.

He nodded toward the television. "I was watching the latest report from KCPD and their Rose Red Rapist task force."

"And that's funny?"

No, he supposed a woman wouldn't find anything amusing about a rapist who'd attacked with impunity for some time now. "It's funny that they're not making any progress on their investigation. They've solved two crimes in the past week, and neither is the one they were investigating."

She stood and took the papers from him. "You're worried, aren't you?"

"About the task force?" Irritated by the presumption, he stood. He would not let a woman—any woman—think she was superior to him. "Why should I care about what the police are doing?"

She set the papers down—in the wrong pile. His heart thudded in his chest.

As if she could hear the pounding sound against his ribs, she rested her palm against his chest, and made a shushing, soothing sound.

Don't believe her, the voice inside his head warned him. *She's a woman. How can you trust a woman?*

How could he not trust this one?

"I know your secrets," she said. His hands curled into fists at his sides. She took care of him in so many ways, knew him so well. He needed her. And that, perhaps, was why he hated her so much. "And I won't let anyone else hurt you. Ever again."

* * * * *

Look for the next exciting book in Julie Miller's
THE PRECINCT: TASK FORCE miniseries
Coming in 2013
Only from Harlequin Intrigue

COMING NEXT MONTH from Harlequin® Intrigue®
AVAILABLE SEPTEMBER 4, 2012

#1371 MASON
The Lawmen of Silver Creek Ranch
Delores Fossen
Deputy Mason Ryland's new horse trainer, Abbie Baker, has some Texas-sized secrets that have put her—and Mason's own family—in the crosshairs of a killer.

#1372 SECRET KEEPER
Cooper Security
Paula Graves
When a wounded warrior discovers an injured woman in his backyard, can he rediscover his inner hero to protect the woman from the dangerous men after her secret?

#1373 INTUITION
Guardians of Coral Cove
Carol Ericson
Psychic Kylie Grant believes in fate. So when she returns to her hometown and winds up working a case with her high school crush Matt Conner, is it fate or folly?

#1374 SCENE OF THE CRIME: BLACK CREEK
Carla Cassidy
When FBI agents Cassie Miller and Mick McCane are assigned undercover to bait a killer, they must overcome baggage from their past and keep each other alive in a deadly game.

#1375 HER BABY'S FATHER
Rebecca York
After Sara Carter's car crashes, a series of events take her back nine months in time to save the man she loves.

#1376 RELENTLESS PROTECTOR
Thriller
Colleen Thompson
With her son taken hostage, Lisa Meador turns to former army ranger Cole Sawyer. Determined to keep the promise he made to Lisa's late husband, Cole will protect her, no matter the consequence.

You can find more information on upcoming Harlequin® titles, free excerpts and more at www.Harlequin.com.

HICNM0812

REQUEST YOUR FREE BOOKS!
2 FREE NOVELS PLUS 2 FREE GIFTS!

Harlequin®

INTRIGUE

BREATHTAKING ROMANTIC SUSPENSE

YES! Please send me 2 FREE Harlequin Intrigue® novels and my 2 FREE gifts (gifts are worth about $10). After receiving them, if I don't wish to receive any more books, I can return the shipping statement marked "cancel." If I don't cancel, I will receive 6 brand-new novels every month and be billed just $4.49 per book in the U.S. or $5.24 per book in Canada. That's a saving of at least 14% off the cover price! It's quite a bargain! Shipping and handling is just 50¢ per book in the U.S. and 75¢ per book in Canada.* I understand that accepting the 2 free books and gifts places me under no obligation to buy anything. I can always return a shipment and cancel at any time. Even if I never buy another book, the two free books and gifts are mine to keep forever.

182/382 HDN FEQ2

Name	(PLEASE PRINT)

Address	Apt. #

City	State/Prov.	Zip/Postal Code

Signature (if under 18, a parent or guardian must sign)

Mail to the **Reader Service:**
IN U.S.A.: P.O. Box 1867, Buffalo, NY 14240-1867
IN CANADA: P.O. Box 609, Fort Erie, Ontario L2A 5X3

Not valid for current subscribers to Harlequin Intrigue books.

**Are you a subscriber to Harlequin Intrigue books
and want to receive the larger-print edition?
Call 1-800-873-8635 or visit www.ReaderService.com.**

* Terms and prices subject to change without notice. Prices do not include applicable taxes. Sales tax applicable in N.Y. Canadian residents will be charged applicable taxes. Offer not valid in Quebec. This offer is limited to one order per household. All orders subject to credit approval. Credit or debit balances in a customer's account(s) may be offset by any other outstanding balance owed by or to the customer. Please allow 4 to 6 weeks for delivery. Offer available while quantities last.

Your Privacy—The Reader Service is committed to protecting your privacy. Our Privacy Policy is available online at www.ReaderService.com or upon request from the Reader Service.

We make a portion of our mailing list available to reputable third parties that offer products we believe may interest you. If you prefer that we not exchange your name with third parties, or if you wish to clarify or modify your communication preferences, please visit us at www.ReaderService.com/consumerschoice or write to us at Reader Service Preference Service, P.O. Box 9062, Buffalo, NY 14269. Include your complete name and address.

HI11B

Harlequin and Mills & Boon are joining forces in a global search for new authors.

In September 2012 we're launching our biggest contest yet—with the prize of being published by the world's leader in romance fiction!

Look for more information on our website, **www.soyouthinkyoucanwrite.com**

So you think you can write? Show us!

*In the newest continuity series from Harlequin®
Romantic Suspense, the worlds of the Coltons and their
Amish neighbors collide—with dramatic results.*

*Take a sneak peek at the first book, COLTON DESTINY
by Justine Davis, available September 2012.*

"**I**'m here to try and find your sister."

"I know this. But don't assume this will automatically ensure trust from all of us."

He was antagonizing her. Purposely.

Caleb realized it with a little jolt. While it was difficult for anyone in the community to turn to outsiders for help, they had all reluctantly agreed this was beyond their scope and that they would cooperate.

Including—in fact, especially—him.

"Then I will find these girls without your help," she said, sounding fierce.

Caleb appreciated her determination. He *wanted* that kind of determination in the search for Hannah. He attempted a fresh start.

"It is difficult for us—"

"What's difficult for me is to understand why anyone wouldn't pull out all the stops to save a child whose life could be in danger."

Caleb wasn't used to being interrupted. Annie would never have dreamed of it. But this woman was clearly nothing like his sweet, retiring Annie. She was sharp, forceful and very intense.

"I grew up just a couple of miles from here," she said. "And I always had the idea the Amish loved their kids just as we did."

"Of course we do."

"And yet you'll throw roadblocks in the way of the people best equipped to find your missing children?"

Caleb studied her for a long, silent moment. "You are very angry," he said.

"Of course I am."

"Anger is an…unproductive emotion."

She stared at him in turn then. "Oh, it can be very productive. Perhaps you could use a little."

"It is not our way."

"Is it your way to stand here and argue with me when your sister is among the missing?"

Caleb gave himself an internal shake. Despite her abrasiveness—well, when compared to Annie, anyway—he could not argue with her last point. And he wasn't at all sure why he'd found himself sparring with this woman. She was an Englishwoman, and what they said or did mattered nothing to him.

Except it had to matter now. For Hannah's sake.

Don't miss any of the books in this exciting
new miniseries from Harlequin® Romantic Suspense,
starting in September 2012 and running
through December 2012.

Copyright © by Janice Davis Smith